# BANTER OF THE DEVIL

## DESIRED BY THE DEVIL
### BOOK 2

## BELLA MOONDRAGON

*For Soni*

# CONTENTS

1

---

# AN UNFORTUNATE ACCIDENT

Bailey

I WATCH the sun gleam off the roof of my car through the window of the breakroom at the Sunshine Clinic, a little urgent care tucked on a busy corner on the outskirts of New Orleans. I check my watch. It's nearly 6:00 P.M., which means my shift is almost over, thank God.

I roll my shoulders and slouch in the creaky, plastic chair, drumming my fingers on the vinyl table top.

Jazzie, a fellow nurse and the clinic manager when the doctors aren't around, walks into the breakroom looking bored and withdrawn. She opens the fridge and pops open a can of diet soda with a heavy sigh. "It's hotter than hell."

"At least it's slow today," I say, glancing at my watch again. It's now 5:57 P.M., just three more minutes....

"Just go, Bailey. None of the doctors are even here right now."

I glance up at Jazzie as she leans against the counter near the fridge and presses the cold soda can to her temple. Her blonde hair is pulled back in a tight bun, and her hairline is peppered with sweat.

"Are you going to stay to wait for the HVAC guy?" I ask, standing and gathering my purse from the back of the chair.

She nods, shrugging. "I don't mind the overtime."

"Okay, cool. I'll see you tomorrow then–"

Her grimace cuts me off.

"About that... you're not on the schedule for the rest of the week."

"Oh," I murmur.

"I'm sorry. I know this is supposed to be a temporary gig, you know. I needed the hours, and we've been so slow lately–"

"Honestly," I say, meeting her hazel eyes with a smile, "It's not a big deal. Just, uh, give me a call if you need shifts covered."

Jazzie nods, giving me a reluctantly smile in return as I make my leave, quickly.

I don't bother gathering my salad dressing and the 12-pack of sports drinks out of the fridge. I've only been working here part-time for three months, and I didn't let myself get comfortable. Jazzie was right about this being a temporary gig. I've been bouncing from urgent care to urgent care, or from assisted living back to urgent care, for almost a year now.

And I'm fucking tired of putting bandages on bruises and sticking IVs in the drunk tourists that hobble their way here from Bourbon Street.

Heat fans over my cheeks as I hurry to my car. Its door handle simmers as I curl my hand around it and yank the door open, wincing at the burn. My leather seats are just as hot, and I make quick work of blasting the AC as high as it can go and rolling down my window, letting the hot air roll out as I rip out of the parking lot and onto the thoroughfare.

I check out my reflection in the rearview mirror while waiting at a stoplight. My normally golden-brown skin is now a deep bronze from the sunny, hotter than expected spring we just had, and the humidity causes my black hair to coil into tight curls around my face. They bounce over my shoulders as I unfasten the claw-clip I use to keep my hair out of my face while I'm working.

The stop light stays red. The people in the cars on either side of me are gesturing, wondering what the holdup is. I tap my fingers on the steering wheel to the music, wondering the same.

It's been a weird year, at least career wise. I could go work in a hospital, of course. I'm more than qualified as an RN.

But I've never liked the sterile, cold atmosphere. The hustle of the urgent care setting is nice, I guess. The days go by quickly, and I'm not tasked with saving anyone's life on a regular basis.

I miss working one-on-one with clients, though. I've been trying to find a more permanent position as an in-home nurse, but it's been slim pickings in Hahnville.

I just need to find a job for another two months, that's it.

Because two months from now, Layla is coming back, and the two of us are going to LSU to get our Nurse Practitioner licenses.

I smile at the memory of Layla. She's been living in Florida for a little under a year now with Dalton, who's been busy with his art restoration business.

I miss Layla. One day, she promised, we're going to start our own practice together. Our very own clinic in New Orleans.

The light finally turns green right at the second my phone rings in my purse.

I blindly fumble through my bag and answer it on the final ring.

"Hello?" I say in a sing-song voice, and I'm met by Helen Wilson's soft chuckle.

"I just love how you answer the phone, honey. How are you?"

"Oh, Hi, Helen. I'm driving and didn't look at the caller ID. I'm fine. Just lost another job."

"Perfect timing."

I snort with laughter. "Is Robert looking for a new checkout girl? I'm pretty good with a keyboard."

She laughs again and says, "No, no. We actually need a nurse."

"Oh?" I make a sharp turn, praying that there's no cops watching me try to hold a phone to my ear while navigating rush hour traffic out of New Orleans proper. "What happened?"

"Robert broke his leg, if you can believe it."

"How did he manage that?"

"He went fishing with a few friends from our church and stepped out of the boat with his leg tangled in a net. He went over the side, snapped his tibia clean in two. It was sticking out of the skin."

"Good lord, Helen! Is he all right?"

"He'll be fine. His ego is crushed, however. He's in the hospital right now for surgery to stick the bone back in."

I wince, turning onto the highway headed toward Hahnville.

"I could use your help. Paid, of course. I'll be picking up his slack at the grocery store until he's back up on his feet."

"Of course! When will he get out of surgery?"

"Soon, I think. He's been in the operating room for an hour. They're going to keep him here for two more days, though, but then he'll be home, laid up. Grouchy as all get out and probably cursing up to the heavens. He's going to be a handful."

I grin then laugh, "Helen, are you hiring me as his nurse or as a babysitter so you get a break from your husband?"

"A bit of both." She laughs, letting out a sigh. "I really appreciate your help, honey. We have an extra bedroom downstairs–"

"I still live in Hahnville," I cut in, laughing. "You don't have to put me up in your house unless you're looking to pay me for night shifts as well."

"Hmm... I feel like I knew this," she says in a coy tone that tells me exactly where this conversation is headed. "Your mom must've said something during the church services you've been avoiding..."

"Because I'm living in sin with my boyfriend?" I laugh. "Mom loves Tanner. Don't let her tell you otherwise. She's also desperate for grandkids."

"I'm just giving you a hard time, Bailey. You'll need to bring that man over for dinner at our house sometime. We see him from afar while he's out at the old Gregory place. He's very handsome."

My smile is soft and knowing. "Yeah, he really is handsome, isn't he?"

Tanner's image flashes through my mind. Soft, dark brown hair that he keeps kind of shaggy. That stubble on his jaw, and his suntanned skin. Big muscles.

Tanner is all *man*. Every inch of him.

I shift in my seat, my thighs rubbing together between the pale blue scrubs I wore to work today. "Call me when Robert is home, okay? I'll come right over."

"You got it, honey. Thank you so much!"

I hang up and toss my phone in the passenger seat just as I edge onto the exit into Hahnville.

The sleepy, small town southwest of New Orleans sits in a haze of sunny humidity, settled on the banks of the Mississippi River.

A few minutes later, I pull into Tanner's driveway–well, our driveway. We've been living together full time for a few months now, but everything still feels fresh and new. When I notice his work truck is nowhere to be seen, I call him, pinching my phone between my shoulder and ear as I fumble with my key set.

"Babe," he says, his voice low and rasping. I can hear a radio in the background punctuated by the swirling hum of power tools.

"Are you still at the old Gregory place?" I ask, pushing open the front door and sighing with relief as the AC chilled air wafts over my skin.

"Yeah... ran into a bit of an issue while framing today. We're running behind. But I don't have to be at the station tonight, so it's just me and you when I get home." Tanner runs his own construction company while also acting as the volunteer fire chief. I really hit the lottery when it comes to blue-collar men.

"So I don't get to see you all dressed up in your uniform?" I tease.

A low, growling laugh wraps me in a warm embrace through the phone. "We'll play later, Bailey. I'm taking my girl out tonight. Wherever you wanna go."

"That seasonal joint by the river just opened back up for the summer," I offer as I walk up the stairs to our bedroom. I hit the speaker button and toss my phone on the bed. "They have crawfish etouffee on the menu."

"God, I love your accent," he groans. "I'm about done here. Put on something tight."

Before he hangs up, I hear a strained, scratching sound coming through the line. It's a song, something familiar, something that sends tremors down my spine. I open my mouth to ask what radio station he's playing in the background, but the call ends with nothing more than a few beeps.

I shrug away that creeping, uneasy sensation. Like I said, it's been a weird year since the fire that changed the trajectory of my life. A year ago, I was standing on the porch at the old Gregory mansion welcoming Layla Bryant into the house where I worked as a day nurse for Miss Penny.

Something changed during those weeks that Layla worked at the house. Something dark bled from the walls and the floorboards, consuming the place, consuming Layla.

But she's never talked to me about it in length. Dalton showed up out of nowhere, her secret artist boyfriend, and then the house simply... burned down.

It's not that it ever felt like a normal house. I've lived in Louisiana my entire life. I've seen and felt things I can't explain. But I never felt threatened by the Gregory property. In fact, I loved it there.

And since the day Tanner wrapped me in a blanket and propped me on the back of his truck to make sure I wasn't dying of smoke inhalation–the very first time we met–I've been floundering.

At least I have Tanner. He's everything good and everything constant in my life.

And I am definitely wearing something tight for him tonight.

I check out my reflection in the mirror, running my hands down the soft, pale cream sundress that hugs my breasts in a way I know will make Tanner drool. I pull my hair back off my slender neck and tie it in a bun with a ribbon.

I feel, for the first time in months, like I can breathe again.

Some say the marsh where all those old plantation homes dwell has spirits that still live there. There's a pull to that place that's hard to ignore.

And in two days, I'll be going back.

Two days, and I'll be a home nurse again.

I hear the garage door open, and Tanner's truck pulls into the driveway. I meet him at the door, and his eyes reach mine before dropping to the ample cleavage I have on display.

I have a feeling we're not leaving for dinner. Not yet.

2

———————

# REBUILDING

Tanner

I WIPE my brow and look down at the scattered, broken power tools lying at my feet. This is the fourth time this has happened in the past month since we started framing. My guys sometimes keep their tools in one of the old outbuildings that survived the fire that destroyed the main house, but lately some strange stuff has been happening.

I look up at Jose, my framer, who's standing with his arms crossed a few feet away. He gives me a shrug.

"You check the cameras?" I ask, motioning to the outbuilding—nothing more than a decaying shed that's probably as old as my grandparents, who are well into their nineties.

"Nothing. Not even a raccoon. And the padlock was still on the door."

I run my tongue along my lower teeth. Shit.

I nudge one of the drills with my foot. It's melted, literally. Like someone threw it into a fire. The yellow plastic is now a charred black, and the rest of the tools aren't in any better shape.

I had cameras installed around the property after the second time this happened, thinking it was a bunch of local kids being idiots. Nothing ever shows up on them to give us a clue as to what's going on.

Beyond the vandalism, other weird stuff has been happening. Tools stop working. The radio the guys carry around will skip to obscure oldies stations with the volume cranked up to the max. Random storms will roll in and rain us out.

I look out over the tree line where the marsh begins. The sun glints off the cemetery back there, just within sight.

"Your tools working today?" I ask Jose, who shakes his head.

"I get a charge on my Dewalt batteries for like five minutes before I have to switch them out. I've been charging them all night at home."

"I know," I reply, nodding absently. What the hell is going on? It's like this place doesn't want a new house built on it, especially one this massive, and frankly, gaudy and pretentious.

I'm making a hell of a lot of money on this contract, however. I want Bailey to have the biggest diamond this side of the Mississippi on her finger come this Christmas.

"I'm going to get an electrician here this week to see if he can get us back on grid. We'll set up some exterior outlets along the foundation base while we're framing," I say, motioning toward the bones of the almost ten-thousand square foot mansion we're building. "I'll buy tools with cords if I have to. We gotta get this beast framed by August if we're going to get back on schedule."

Jose just nods, looking as frustrated as I am.

But then a pearly white Lexus tears into the driveway, and both of us curse under our breath.

Jake, the new owner of the Gregory property, gets out his car looking like he just walked off the greens. His khaki shorts and pale pink golf shirt are spotless as he glances around and pushes his sunglasses down the bridge of his nose.

Here we fucking go.

"What the hell, Tanner?"

"Nice to see you, Jake," I grumble, tucking my hands in the pockets of my jeans as I walk in his direction.

"Yeah," he practically growls. He waves a hand toward the beginnings of his future home with a sneer. "What am I looking at?"

"Framing."

"Ah, looks totally livable."

"You realize how long it takes to build a house bigger than the local high school, right?"

Jake glowers at me for another second before pushing his sunglasses back up the bridge of his nose and crossing his arms over his chest, heaving a sigh.

"The wife is on my ass. All of my money is going toward this, and she wants to take a vacation."

"Didn't you just get back from vacation?"

Jake shrugs, sniffing. "What's the smell? Is something burning?"

"I don't smell anything."

Jake looks around, watching the crew of ten guys I have working on the framing portion of this job. I told Jake I'd have it fully framed by July, and it's June. Despite the mishaps with the tools, we're still somewhat on track.

But Jake is young, dumb, and rich. There's a lot of people like him flooding the old towns lining the Mississippi River, buying up all the old plantation properties and building shit like this.

Modern. Sparkling. All sharp corners and big windows. None of the charm Hahnville is known for.

"Look, Jake. This house is enormous, plus you wanted the five car garage finished first. We're on track, but we've been running into vandalism issues again. I wanted to talk to you about putting in a new gate at the start of the driveway and hiring a security guard or two to walk the grounds at night–"

Jake waves a hand, cutting me off. "Do whatever. I don't care. I just want this place finished so I can put it on the market. The wife wants to buy a place in Miami now." Jake's phone rings, and his tone changes the second he answers it. Suddenly, he's chipper and charismatic as he walks to his car and gets inside.

He peels out, kicking up dust.

I shake my head, watching him speed off down the driveway, the low hanging cypress trees swallowing his car from view.

*Do whatever....* Fine. This man doesn't care how much money he's spending on construction as long as he can sell the house for triple what he spent on it.

I remind myself this is just a job as I get back to work. But I've always had a thing for these old properties. I love the architecture, the charm. I love the way the marsh hugs the property line and how the cicadas sing their song when the sun starts to go down.

One day, I want a house on the river like this. I want to bring one of those old houses back to its former glory.

I want to sit out on a screened back porch with Bailey while our kids catch frogs at sunset, and fall asleep beside her while rain patters against reclaimed windows.

That's why I continue to take jobs like this.

Admittedly, however, the Gregory property gives me the creep. The house that sat here before had none of the charm I'm hoping for and every ounce of foreboding like something out of a slasher film.

"The radio's acting up again, boss," one of the framers says.

"I'll add that to the list," I reply testily.

Hours pass, and somehow, my crew gets the entire second floor framed. I'm packing up to leave, instructing my crew to just take their tools home to be on the safe side. The sticky note in my pocket is full of notes about who to call about security guards and a new electronic gate out front, and that's honestly the best I can do.

I watch my crew leave, but I linger.

It's sunset. I have to start a three day shift at the firehouse tonight. Bailey is home getting ready to start a nursing gig for the neighbors, Helen and Robert.

I have nowhere to be right now, so I sit on the foundation and take a deep breath.

I look up at the frames of what's eventually going to be a four story home. Maybe Jake will let me bring in some contractors to help bring some character to this modern style behemoth. I can imagine the house as something else with the same bones–something grand and colorful, dripping with character, and worth every penny of the four million dollars Jake thinks he's going to get for it when it's done.

Even with my successful business, I could never afford a house like this. Not here. Not with all the rich folk moving out of New Orleans seeking more land to stake a claim to.

Frogs are making a racket in the tree line as the sun dips below the horizon, casting the area in a deep violet glow.

I turn my head toward the cemetery–which Jake has been fighting with the historical society about removing–and notice someone standing there among the headstones.

I rub my eyes, thinking they're playing tricks on me.

I don't believe in ghosts. I never have. I'm not a religious man either. I firmly believe there's a logical explanation to everything.

When I look back at the cemetery, it's empty.

I go straight from the job site to the firehouse. I shower and get in bed, rolling over onto my side and plugging in my phone. I text Bailey, telling her I love her, and that she should come by the firehouse for dinner tomorrow if she has a chance.

But as I send the text, it bounces back. The service bars on my phone cut out, and so does the power.

Ronnie, one of the firefighters, sits up in the cot he's been lying in for a while now.

I sit up as well, listening in the sudden, total silence. A clicking noise sounds in the utility room directly below us, and then the backup generator kicks on.

It's a clear, still night. No storms to worry about.

"Weird," Ronnie says, lying back down.

"I'll go check it out," I groan, getting out of bed.

I walk down to the utility room. Nothing is amiss, and the generator is working properly. I walk out into the street next. There's definitely a power outage. Hahnville is cloaked in darkness as I edge back onto the sidewalk with a sigh. I should call Bailey and make sure she's okay. I don't like the idea of her being in the house all alone when it's so dark.

I turn toward the firehouse and catch movement out of the corner of my eye. It's just someone walking on the sidewalk away from me—a man in a strange coat—something dated, almost like a costume.

I watch him walk around a corner and out of sight before going back to bed.

3

___________________

# MORE DARK SECRETS

Bailey

HELEN AND ROBERT'S house has always been bright and homey. It smells like roses as I step inside, breathing deeply. Helen's wallpapered formal living room glistens–spotless and freshly dusted. The kitchen is on the other side of the foyer, as well as a dining room and small washroom.

The layout is similar to the old Gregory house. All of the old houses were built like this–every room contained, connected by archways and built around a grand foyer with a sweeping staircase.

But comparatively, Helen and Robert's house is much smaller and cozier, as is their heavily wooded property.

Helen pours glasses of sweet tea. "He's upstairs in bed," she sighs, sipping from her glass. "He's still coming off the drugs. I was told he'd be woozy for a day or two."

"Is he on any pain medication?"

"He has a nerve blocker in his chest right now. Robert doesn't do well on the heavy duty pain killers they prescribed. They make him sick to his stomach."

"He might be all right with something over the counter if we can keep him comfortable."

Helen smiles at me a bit wistfully. "It's his ego that's in the most pain, I think. He won't really tell me the details of what happened. I didn't even know he was going fishing that evening."

I follow her into the dining room where we sit down across from one another. I go through his discharge paperwork from the hospital and chat lightly with Helen over the chilled glasses of tea, making notes of his best course of care.

"The nerve blocker will run out of medicine in a few days, so until then, I'll just be doing after care." I glance down at the extra notes from the surgeon I had Helen request. Had I not been able to take this job, Robert would have spent another week or more in the hospital before being moved to a rehab facility.

The break is... far worse than Helen made it sound. I don't think Tylenol is going to cut it.

I notice the prescription for some next level pain meds and sigh. I need to keep this somewhere I can find it. I have a feeling Robert is going to need it.

His left leg is all screws and metal now.

Helen looks exhausted, too. Dark circles line her eyes as she balances her head on her hand and slumps her shoulders.

"Long first night home?" I ask, and she nods, stifling a yawn.

"He's uncomfortable. My sister is going to drive down from New Orleans for the next few weekends to help, but I didn't get a wink of sleep last night."

I lean back in my chair and cross my arms under my chest. "Let's set him up in the guest room for now. He's going to be bedridden for a while, Helen. He can't use his leg at all, and he doesn't start physical therapy for another three weeks. He won't be up and moving until then, and I'm going to have to..." I taper off. Something feels strange about this. This is a major break, a violent one, at that. How the hell was he able to do this by falling out of an airboat? "You need sleep, and I have a feeling Robert is going to be most active at night for a while. That's going to be when he's the most uncomfortable. I don't know why, but that's just the way it is." I wave my hand in dismissal. Human bodies are weird.

"You don't have to work nights, honey," she says, but I shake my head.

"Helen, you weigh a little over a hundred pounds, I'm guessing. If he needs to go to the bathroom, how are you going to pick him up, get him in a wheelchair, pick him up again so he can–"

She huffs a breath. "You're right."

"He'll be using a bedpan for a while anyway. Wouldn't you rather have your own space during that time?"

She grimaces. "I understand. I just hate having you on such a strange schedule."

"Don't worry about me. Tanner has that big job next door and sleeps at the firehouse four nights a week anyway. He wasn't happy about me being home alone in the house when the power went out the other night. I think he'll feel better about me being here, with you guys, while he's on shift."

She smiles softly. "Tanner sounds like a nice man."

"He's the best," I agree. He really is. Kind, brave, and gentle. He's everything I imagined a partner should be. And, he loves me. Like really, really just adores me and worships the ground I walk on. Growing up, I had a few boyfriends. I had one that liked to rough me up a little just to see me squirm. I hated that, but I stayed because I was young and naive.

I swore off dating for a long time after that.

Falling into Tanner's arm was serendipitous, to say the least. My life changed the day I met him.

I miss him, suddenly, but I'll see him tomorrow morning, I'm sure.

Upstairs, a low groan alerts us that Robert is awake.

Helen stands, but I motion for her to stop. "Seriously, Helen. Go get some sleep. I'll get Robert comfortable again and go up to New Orleans to pick up his medications in case he changes his mind and some supplies. I'll get the guest room set up later, and we'll move him over there tonight so you can get a full night's rest."

"I'll whip something up for dinner in a few hours," she says, yawning. "I think I'll take a cat nap in the sunroom for a while."

"I'll wake you up if I need anything."

That seems to make her feel better about her decision to leave me in charge and treat me like the help I am instead of a guest.

I pad up the stairs to the master suite and find Robert groaning in bed. Shutting the door behind me with a smile stretched across my lips, I say, "Good morning, sunshine."

"Oh, Christ," he grunts. "What are you doing here?"

"Are you not happy to see me?"

Robert rolls his eyes and tries to get into a seated position. I rush to him, ignoring his attempts to wave me away.

"I'm your nurse for the foreseeable future, Robert. Let me do my job."

"I'm sure Helen and I can't afford you, Bailey."

I wink at him. "I cut your wife a deal."

Another roll of his eyes, but he seems more comfortable sitting up. His gaze, however, is a bit hazy still. He's coming down from a ton of medication. It might be a few more days until he's fully lucid, and that's when the real work will start.

"Can I get you anything?"

"A gun."

"Why?" I laugh, but Robert isn't amused.

"So I can shoot myself in the head for putting my wife through this."

I nod, feeling sorry for the man. Robert is like Tanner, in my opinion. He dotes on Helen. She is the brightest light in his life, and the idea of her having to take care of him is weighing him down significantly.

I sit on the edge of bed. "Look, Robert. I sent Helen to take a nap.

I'm going to be helping out as much as I can, all right? Don't feel bad about what happened. Helen is strong and just worried about making sure you're comfortable." I reach over and clutch his hand, giving it a little squeeze. "I'll take care of her too, I promise."

He looks toward the window. In the distance, over the treetops, I can just see the faint outline of the massive house being built on the Gregory property.

He's looking right at it, a far off look in his eyes.

I feel uneasy as I release his hands. He's cold and clammy, another side effect of coming off enough pain meds to take down a horse. I walk to the closet and pull out a few quilts Helen made and start laying them over his lap.

"Robert," I say after several minutes of uneasy silence, "how did this happen?"

He swallows. Shirtless, I can see the nerve blocker sticking to his chest, a little tube poking out under the tape keeping it in place. It's feeding slow release painkillers into his system as we speak.

"A boat."

"No, that wasn't it," I whisper, and he turns to look at me.

His eyes are milky in the sunlight–bloodshot and hazy.

"Don't tell Helen."

"I won't," I promise. I'm not sure why I want to know so badly, but his leg is crushed, not just broken. He'll be walking with a limp for the rest of his life. I'm honestly shocked, based on the doctor's notes about the surgery, that they didn't amputate his leg instead.

Helen doesn't understand the medical lingo and codes, but I do.

This was a terrible, horrific accident, and Robert is lucky to be alive.

"I walked over to the Gregory property a few nights ago," he admits. "I took the trail through the marsh. I like to go out there to fish. You can get to the river, you know, if you go far enough. But I ended up on the Gregory side, close to the cemetery. I keep looking at the new house being built through this window and thought I might as well try to get a closer look."

My stomach hollows out as his voice drops. Fear punctuates every syllable before he can brush it away as he continues, "It started raining real hard. I couldn't get a view, so I walked up onto the cemetery plot and I... it gets real hazy after that. I think I might have fallen in a grave."

"What?" I choke out. That's impossible. No one has been buried there for decades. There wouldn't be an open, freshly dug grave there right now. Not that I know of.

He nods but then shakes his head after a moment. "I woke up miles away, soaking wet. I got pulled out of the water by some fishermen who thought I was dead already, and they got me to the hospital."

I watch him as he looks back toward the window.

"I've always gotten a bad feeling about that place. I don't know how you worked there for so long."

I swallow hard. "It's not so bad."

"Have you spoken to Layla in a while?"

"We talk every week on the phone," I tell him, trying to find a smile to give him, but a ripple of gooseflesh makes the hair on the back of my neck stand up.

"You should check on her," he says quietly before closing his eyes. He falls asleep almost instantly.

Now, I'm really feeling strange. Layla has never spoken to me about how the fire happened. Neither of us have any idea where Vera is. She hasn't been seen or heard from in a year.

Why would Robert want me to check on her all of the sudden?

I ease him onto his back and spend the next hour checking out his wound, cleaning around the screws jutting from his swollen, bruised skin. I go downstairs and check on Helen, who is fast asleep on the couch in the sunroom. I make another batch of sweet tea for her to wake up to, setting the pitcher in the sunny kitchen window to steep.

Then I get back in my car and drive to New Orleans, and once I cross out of Hahnville, that feeling of creeping, insatiable unease finally lifts.

But Robert's words are imprinted in my mind.

What exactly happened at the Gregory property?

And why was I left in the dark about it?

4

———————————

## SNEAKING SUSPICIONS

Tanner


BAILEY SINGS to the radio over the sound of the faucet, her hands shielded by pink rubber gloves dotted with white daisies. Rain patters the windows in the kitchen as I set a few dishes down next to the sink, smiling down at my girlfriend.

God, she's beautiful, and I'm one lucky son-of-a-bitch to have her here.

I came home from the job site today to find her in the kitchen up to her elbows in dinner preparations. Cornbread, mashed potatoes with gravy, breaded pork chops, and creamed spinach.

I remember the first time I brought her back to my place. I'd offered to cook her dinner to try to impress her, but I only knew how to make spaghetti with sauce from a jar. So, we ate that, and steak. And the next night, at her old apartment, she made me some type of pasta dish with chicken that had me seeing stars and planning our future together.

I count my blessings every day, and she's always at the very top of that list.

"There's plenty leftover if you're still hungry." She grins at me as she scrubs out the pans she used.

I start loading up the dishwasher. "I couldn't eat another bite if I tried. I'll pack the rest for lunch tomorrow."

"What about dessert?" She winks at me, her cheeks going ruddy as she blushes.

I straighten up, closing the dishwasher before leaning against the counter. "Dessert? You know I'm not a sweets man."

"You think I'm sweet." She's flirting with me, and the heated look she's sending my way me gives me immediate tunnel vision. I take a single step toward her, gently grabbing her arm.

I slowly slide the gloves from her fingers and toss them into the sink.

"Tell me about your day, and then I'll consider what I want for dessert," I say, wrapping my arms around her waist and pulling her close. We rock to the jazz music playing on the radio across the room.

"I told you about the Wilsons," she teases. "What more do you want to know?"

"You seemed stressed when you got home."

She steps away, shrugging, and turns back to the unfinished dishes.

"Don't worry about the dishes, Bailey. I'll do them later. Talk to me."

"You'll think I'm crazy."

I narrow my eyes at her. "What's going on?"

"I just... you know how Helen told me he fell out of a boat?"

I nod, sitting down in one of the dining chairs at the table. She sits beside me, sighing deeply.

"I saw Robert and talked to him for a minute, and he told me he didn't break his leg on a fishing trip. He hadn't been fishing at all. I had my suspicions, given how intense his surgery was and how much recovery time he's looking at, but seeing his wound and reading the surgery notes.... He's lucky to be alive."

"How did he do it?"

"He told me was walking through the marsh and ended up in the cemetery near your job site."

My blood runs cold. "He's an old man. He shouldn't have been out there alone."

"I agree, but he knows the marsh. And he's familiar with the Gregory property, seeing as they've lived next door for several decades now. He... he said he fell into a grave."

I chuckle, surprised. "They're no open graves. Nobody's been buried there for a very long time, from what I know."

"I know, that's what makes this so weird. Even worse, he says he passed out and came to along the banks of the river, several miles away, and got picked up by some fishermen and taken to the hospital."

I lean back in my chair and watch Bailey's face undergo a variety of changes. She looks stressed, and I reach out and tug on her arm. "Come here."

She glides over and straddles my lap.

"If you're uncomfortable working there, don't."

"I need a job, Tanner. You know I'm saving up for my nurse practitioner program this fall."

"I have enough money for the two of us."

"You just want to keep me home in an apron, making you apple pie."

"Mm... I love seeing you in an apron." She giggles, but I'm being serious. "If you don't want to work there, say the word. You can spend the summer studying, or doing an internship, or just hanging out. You don't need a job as long as I'm around."

"How did I get such a good man?" she whispers, running her fingers through my hair.

I pull her down and kiss her soundly, enjoying her weight on my lap and the way she drags her tongue over mine. I truly can't get enough of her. I don't think it's possible to stop wanting her every second of every day, but lately that's taken on new heights.

I pick her up and carry her upstairs into our bedroom, not bothering to shut the door behind us as I sit on the edge of the bed and continue the kiss.

Lately, I've been having daydreams about her. About her walking to me, naked, moonlight highlighting every curve and angle of her body as she leans over me, whispering the dirtiest things I've ever heard in my ear.

The woman in my dreams isn't the sweet, kind Bailey I know.

It still makes me hard at awkward hours of the day, though.

I tug on her tank top straps, pulling them down over her shoulders. She's not wearing a bra, and her breasts bounce free—full and heavy in my hands.

She pushes me back against the mattress and starts unbuttoning my shirt, and I lie there underneath her, letting her take control.

She's like a drug to me, and I will do anything to get my next fix, but I'm gentle with her. She likes that—that quiet passion, and so do I.

Things have always been easy and natural between us. I guess this is how it's supposed to feel when you finally meet your person.

But lately I've been... wanting to do other things, things I wouldn't have thought about doing to her before.

Not hurting her exactly, but pushing some limits, seeing how far I can make her body go....

I snap out of it, feeling like I'm trapped in someone else's thoughts.

"Bailey," I rasp against her neck before flipping her over onto her back. She giggles as she hits the mattress, and I quickly pull off her shirt and help her shimmy out of her shorts and wet panties. I run my hands down her sides, over the curve of her waist and her perfect thighs.

My mouth waters, and my cock is hard and aching against the fly of my jeans.

I let out a groan of satisfaction as she unzips my pants and tries to shove them down my hips.

"In a hurry tonight?" I whisper against her neck, nibbling the tender skin there. I love her neck. Slender, delicate. I'm obsessed with it, and I love when she wears her bounty of hair up so I can see it.

I kick off my jeans, pull my boxers down, and nudge her legs apart.

Her pussy is divine as I slide into her, feeling her muscles hugging my cock tight enough my breath catches in my throat.

She whimpers my name, her eyes fluttering closed. God, she's an angel.

And I want her at my mercy....

I shake my head, feeling suddenly... off kilter. It's like someone is whispering in my ear, telling me to... to take her. To lay claim to what's mine and to forget about the repercussions.

"*Oh, my god,*" she moans, gripping my thighs as I rock my hips against her, her wet pussy squeezing around my cock. "Tanner–"

I thrust into her hard, and she squeaks, which makes my cock even harder, if that's possible.

"Do that again," she moans, and I do, slamming into her with enough force that the headboard cracks against the wall. She arches her hips and cries out.

I pull out and flip her over onto her stomach, gripping her hands and yanking her so she's resting on her knees.

Leaning over her, I brush her hair away from her neck and plant a rough kiss to the top of her spine, my teeth grazing her skin.

I slam into her again, slapping her ass, losing the grip I had on reality in the process. I clutch her neck, my fingers tightening around her throat, and she lets out a surprised gasp that stops me in my tracks.

I slowly pull out and tease her clit with the head of my cock while testing my grip on her throat.

"Do you like that?" I ask, slowly pressing my dick inside her soaked pussy, inch by inch.

"Y-yes–" she gasps.

I tighten my grip again, loving the way she jerks and grinds her hips into mine.

Fuck, I have full control of her. I have control of her pleasure, and her very breath.

I slap her ass until her skin turns bright red, and she screams my name, her pussy spasming around my cock.

I come, hard, spilling into her, and hold myself there.

Slowly, I pull out and roll her over onto her back again, kissing her tenderly, but Bailey is giving me an odd look as I lean away.

"What?" I ask, noticing the marks on her neck and wondering... "Bailey, I'm sorry."

She touches her neck, and I immediately feel like shit. "It's okay. I–I liked it."

"Are you sure?"

She nods, but there's a strange feeling growing in my stomach, something uneasy and....

I get off the bed and pull my boxers on. "I love you," I tell her, holding her gaze. "If I hurt you–"

"You didn't hurt me," she smiles, rising up and balancing her weight on her elbows. "I liked it. I like you... unleashed, sometimes."

I smile, but deep down, I feel like shit.

"I'm going to go do those dishes now."

"I'm gonna read for a bit."

"All right." I slip out of the room and curse on my way downstairs. We've gotten kinky, sure. I'd folded her over the bed of my truck a time or two, but choking her out?

As I round the corner of the kitchen, the radio shuts off on its own.

I look around and wonder if I'm not entirely alone right now.

"Hello?" I say to the empty kitchen.

But like usual, there's no one there.

5

---

# DARKNESS SETS IN

Bailey


THE WILSON HOUSE is fairly small, snug, and full of memories.

I love old houses like these. Every creak step and notch in the floorboards holds a memory, and for the Wilsons, that's over three decades of marriage and cohabitation.

I run my finger over the squeaky clean mantle above the seldom used fireplace. I'm sure it's just for show. I can't imagine needing a fire *ever* in a state like Louisiana, but I sure do like the idea of cozying up in front of a fireplace and reading a book on a cold, snowy winter night.

I chuckle to myself at the thought of snow–having never seen it in real life–and go about my business.

I've set up a little workstation in the study off the living room, which is nothing more than a desk, a crammed bookshelf, and a large safe that takes up most of the tiny room. Robert likes to hunt and fish, and it shows. I eye the boxes of bullets, thankful they're covered in years' worth of dust, as I sit down at the cluttered desk and search for Robert's file in my tote bag.

Sighing, I study his surgery notes for the hundredth time, trying to make sense of the trauma to his leg. It doesn't make sense to me. This couldn't have been caused by a fall... maybe from fifty feet in the air, but I doubt the old man is in the habit of climbing trees.

I run my fingers through my hair and glance out the window. I have a view of the marsh, and it's a cloudless, moonlit night. In the distance, I can see the joists connecting the freshly framed third floor at the new Gregory house, and my mind drifts to Tanner.

I had him look over Robert's X-ray. He reviewed the surgery notes as well.

His reaction was so strange... especially for a first responder. He's seen injuries worse than this out in the field as the fire chief and told me all about them with marked enthusiasm.

I'm not squeamish, but this....

I rub my eyes. I'm not used to working night shifts, and this is my first overnight at the Wilson house. Helen went to bed an hour ago in the master suite while Robert is asleep in the guest room.

I wonder how Layla filled the sleepy downtime during her long nights at the old house. Being awake while the rest of the world sleeps is an odd sensation that wraps itself around me like a snake slithering over my skin. Every echo of pipes and soft brush of the cypress trees gliding over the metal roof sounds... different. Wholly changed in the moonlight. It's like I've walked into a different realm, a different space and time entirely.

I need to stop reading fantasy books, I think.

Another rub of my eyes and my legs start to twitch. I need to move, or I'll fall asleep, so I walk throughout the first floor, then the second, checking on Robert before making my way downstairs an hour later to do... whatever.

I end up on the back porch sipping a diet soda, letting the caffeine seep through my veins.

My mom used to tell me stories about the marshes. She used to whisper about the spirits who clung to the wetlands, waiting for a final tide to rush them away to eternal peace.

And, she spoke of the demons who haunted the shallow waters. Demons who preyed on those reckless enough to travel too far into the wetlands.

I smile to myself as I watch the fireflies dart through the bushes at the edge of the yard. This place—this marshy area of the Mississippi—has been my home forever, but tonight I'm seeing it in a new light.

I believe in ghosts, but not the demons Mom talks about. Her stories are the same told generation after generation to keep children from getting lost or eaten by alligators.

Night time here is... serene. It's just me and the fireflies.

I sip my soda as I walk along the edge of the yard with my bare toes in the cool grass. This is a rare kind of summer night. Warm, yes. Still and humid? Of course. But there's a slight, uncommon chill in the air that makes all of the downy soft hair on my body stand on end in the best way as I skirt the property line.

I'm several hundred yards away from the back porch when something large skitters away through the encroaching woods, and I halt.

Helen has been complaining about the racoons and opossums. I used to leave crackers and stale cookies out on the back porch at the Gregory place for them. It was my little secret.

I turn back to the house, but movement catches my attention through the trees, and I pause.

A gentle breeze ripples through me, sending a chill licking down my spine. From where I'm standing, I can just make out a slight incline where the marsh begins. Moonlight reflects off the water as my gaze sweeps over the marsh and up the rise, where I can just make out the outlines of the cemetery.

I hadn't realized how close the Wilsons live to Penny's old place.

The headstones are just a shimmer of gray in the moonlight against a sea of deep, endless greenery, but there's something else.

My spine locks up, and my shoulders square on their own accord as someone walks between the headstones. They're nothing more than a shadow, but I swear... I swear there's someone running their hands over the top edge of each stone as they move in like a ghost.

A twig snaps behind me and I whirl.

"Oh, honey! I didn't mean to startle you!" Helen holds her hands out, her lips pulling back in a cringe. "I thought you might have been sleepwalking!"

"Helen, I'm sorry," I rush out, seeing the panicked look behind her eyes shifting to guilt. "I'm just trying to stay awake. I thought a stroll might do the trick."

"Well, I'm having trouble sleeping myself and had the same idea, though I don't ever walk out this far at night."

She glances around nervously, letting out a shuddering breath. I look over my shoulder at the cemetery.

Maybe it was just a shadow because the figure I thought I saw is no longer there.

"You never walk in the marsh?"

"Oh, of course I do. I like to go and sit by the river sometimes, especially if Robert takes me out while he's fishing, but never along the boundary between our house and the old Gregory property."

"Why not?" I ask, following her as she turns around and rubs her arms like she caught a chill.

"Oh, no reason other than it's always given me the creeps. The marsh just seems darker on that side, more wild."

"Hmm, I suppose you're right."

"Did you walk outside often when you worked for Miss Penny?" We walk back to the house together.

"Not really. Sometimes, if the weather was mild, I'd sit out in the backyard with a book if she was having a particularly calm day, but I never...." I think about it for a moment. "Can I be honest with you?"

She nods, sitting down in the swinging chair on the back porch.

I lean against the porch railing and heave a breath, trying to organize the strange feelings I sometimes had while working in the old house.

"The Gregory property has a bit of edge to it, doesn't it? I mean, some days, when it was just me and Miss Penny, I'd go downstairs to the kitchen to make myself some lunch, and I felt like–like I wasn't entirely alone."

"Mmm…" Helen hums, nodding her head.

"And… When Layla started working there, I felt that feeling even more. Like I wasn't ever alone. Like I could look over my shoulder and find someone–something watching me from afar."

"What did that feel like to you?" Helen asks calmly.

"That's an odd question." I chuckle, shrugging. "I guess… it didn't feel threatening. Maybe… bored curiosity? That changed, though, when all the weird things started happening to Layla, and when we found out what Vera was doing to Miss Penny it got worse." Chills erupt all over my skin. I shake them away. "Do you believe in ghosts, Helen?"

"Oh, of course. You can't live in the deep south without holding some belief about the spirits that linger here."

"Is your house haunted?" I ask, wiggling my eyebrows in her direction.

She smiles, but doesn't laugh. "No. Not all the time. Spirits of all kinds pass through these parts on occasion. I've had weird things happen over the years. I had one spirit of a child that liked to mess with my balls of yarn. But nothing like–nothing like what lived at the Gregory house."

I watch her closely. Her eyes undergo a great change as she sighs, toying with her wedding ring.

She licks her lips, her eyes sliding to mine. "Did Layla tell you anything?"

"About?"

"About… the house?"

"She would ask me if it was haunted. I thought maybe the night shifts were getting to her, like the last night nurse who ran out–"

"I want you to promise me something, Bailey."

"Of course," I say, catching an uncommon edge of desperation in

Helen's voice. She's normally bubbly and chipper, the epitome of southern hospitality, but now?

Real fear shines behind her eyes for a split second as she says, "Do not step foot on the Gregory property ever again."

"Why?"

"Just promise. That place is... scarred. It's the deepest kind of scar, I'm afraid. I don't think you're safe there. And don't go to the cemetery, either. Promise me—"

"I promise," I tell her, even though I'm sure I'm not understanding her sudden insistence. I worked there for years. "I don't have a reason to, anyway. Tanner prefers to pack his own lunch."

She smiles at me, but it's fleeting.

"That scary old house burned down, anyway," I tease, trying to lighten her mood. Had something happened to her there? Does she know something I don't?

"I'm not sure that matters," she whispers to herself.

"What?"

The buzzer I gave Robert to alert me if he needed anything causes an alarm to chime on my watch. I flinch, startled by the synthetic sounds against the calming, hushed lullaby of the swamp.

"You should try to get some rest," I tell Helen as I walk through the back door. But she's not looking at me. Her gaze is resting on the far edge of their backyard, the same place I'd been standing when I caught a glimpse of the cemetery.

I ignore the nagging sensation in my brain that has been telling me to run... for years.

For years, since the moment I crossed the threshold of Miss Penny's front door.

"Goodnight, Bailey," Helen says, and her voice sounds... different. Lower, and more severe.

"Goodnight," I whisper, bristling.

I remind myself I don't believe in the stories my mom told me as a child, but if there are demons in those wetlands... Well, the Gregory property might be full of them.

6

———————

# IMPERFECTIONS

Tanner

JOSE and the rest of the crew have been sitting around kicking rocks for days. That's just how things go, but this house has been the bane of my existence all summer. Once we clear this inspection, work can start up again, but it's taken weeks to even get to this point.

I scan the behemoth of a house, finally able to see the shape taking form. It'll be beautiful when it's done, sure. I'll make certain of that. While I'm not a fan of modern homes, I'll leave my mark on this one as best I can. It'll be the best damn modern home in all of Hahnville.

Storm clouds funnel overhead as I walk around the house, checking the work we've done. It's fully framed now, thank god. I've replaced every single fucking tool since we started building the foundation in the spring.

Jake is finally off my ass about the schedule. It sounds like his wife is changing her tune about living here, which means he's more involved in making this a home rather than a shell made of white and gray walls to sell when we're done.

He wants it done right and done well. I can do that.

As long as whatever demon who hates power tools stops fucking with my jobsite.

I quit smoking years ago, but the scent of menthol makes my skin prickle with a sudden desire to take a drag as I walk into the backyard, which is nothing more than raw earth with a huge hole where a swimming pool will be in the coming weeks.

"We got the inspector coming any minute now," I say to the man leaning against the framed back porch. His back is to me as I come to a stop, tucking my hands in the front pockets of my jeans.

His body is cast in shadow as the clouds take on a greenish shade, threatening a downpour that will push this inspection back... again.

"If you're gonna smoke, go to the tree line. The last thing I need is the inspector thinking I let y'all smoke and drink on the job while using power tools."

A soft, distant chuckle rings through my ears. It sends a chill down my spine as I turn my gaze from the tree line to the man standing near the porch, but...

"Hello?" I call out. "Hey!"

A warm, wet breeze rushes through the trees, disturbing the birds taking shelter from the incoming storm in the shadow of the marsh.

The breeze carries the smell of cigarette smoke, and I feel my stomach curl with a sensation of fear and disgust.

Fucking ghosts. My crew already thinks this place is haunted, and the more time I spend here, the more I think they're right.

"Hey, boss!" someone calls from the front of the house. "Inspector's here for ya!"

I scan the backyard, the tree line, and allow my gaze to graze over the distant, shadow cloaked marsh. The cemetery gleams in the green-hued light.

But there's no one out there.

The guy I saw in the shadows was probably just one of my guys, nothing more. Nothing sinister, like my body seems to think.

I know better, honestly. I grew up just outside of Hahnville in one of the many small towns along the river. I just roamed the wetlands as a boy, disregarding my mother's warnings and sordid stories about the creatures that called the marshes on the banks of the Mississippi home.

That's all it was, though. Stories. Tall tales. Fairy tales. The stuff of childhood dreams.

But there's something about this place that I don't like. I can feel it every time I'm here, and now that Bailey's working at the Wilson place next door, I know she feels it too.

Thankfully, it's Friday. I'll have the whole weekend at home, and Bailey will be by my side.

I skirt around the house, making a last minute sweep of the work we've done, before coming face to face with the inspector.

"Mornin'," I say to Randy Ellsworth, a rat-faced man from New Orleans with a chip on his shoulder almost as big as the clipboard in his meaty hands.

"Looking like a fine morning at that," he says sarcastically as he glances up at the dark clouds choking the sky.

"I say we have about fifteen minutes before it starts to rain, so let's get this over with." I huff, waving him along as I walk up the front porch.

Randy follows me like the little dog he is, and I begin my grand tour.

"You do some good work, Tanner," Randy says ten minutes later as he looks up into the second and third floor rafters. "I'm guessing the OSHA inspector has been here a few times, based on harnesses and other safety apparatuses you got lying around."

"I don't fuck with OSHA, and I especially don't fuck with workers comp."

Randy chuckles, nodding. "Fine work. You passed, but I'm guessing you already knew that would happen."

"This is just the formality I needed to get out of the way before the next phase of work begins."

Randy and I walk back through the first floor of the house. He pauses in what will one day be the kitchen just as rain starts to patter against the concrete beneath our feet. "Thick foundation, I'll tell you what."

"I had the foundation reinforced as best we could, given this place seems to be sinking into the wetlands."

"That wasn't a bad call. I've failed a few inspections further down the river because of sinking foundations. All those old houses are falling into the marshes, getting swallowed whole, like the wetlands want to erase them from history."

"You talk like the wetlands are a living thing."

"Oh, they are! You don't think so?"

"I don't mess with it," I tell him, thinking of Robert Wilson's ill-fated walk through the marshes.

Randy eyes the framing throughout the kitchen as he says, "You've heard the old stories about this place, I assume?"

"Bits and pieces."

"Ah, well... I had the pleasure of sitting in on a meeting of Hahnville's historical society recently, just last week. They're debating your client's request to have the old graves in that cemetery dug up and moved to the cemetery at Hahnville Baptist, you know. And boy... some folks were beside themselves about the sanctity of it, calling it a crime against the dead to those bodies dug up from their eternal rest. But a few mentioned all the deaths here, all the supposed murders over the decades."

I chuckle. "Murders? What, ole Miss Penny was out here luring folks to her big house and killing them from her bed?"

Randy gives me a narrowed look. "No, Tanner. Murders spanning the last century or more. Lots of weird things that can't be explained, at least from what I heard. It sounds like the society was more than willing to let this place go to a private seller when she died instead of having to take care of it themselves. One guy mentioned not wanting to set foot here, and another echoed that, saying the place was the most haunted property in all of Hahnville."

"Yeah, so what? Does this mean I can expect a crew out here to start taking apart the cemetery while my men are working on the house?"

"Possibly. Honestly, it's likely. I know your client has been wanting to have the marsh drained to the property line to expand his backyard, and that boundary is just past the cemetery itself. So, nothing's getting done on that front until the state and feds decide if he can mess with the wetlands, you know."

I nod, reaching up to adjust my baseball cap so the rain stops hitting me in the face. "Are we good here, then?"

"Yeah. Like I said, you passed." He starts to walk out but places a hand on the wall in the hallway where the studs are still a little farther apart than usual. I thought we'd fixed that "This is a little odd though. These studs are an usual width apart. You got a plan, here?"

I make an excuse. "Client wants some sort of closet here. We're still working on it."

Randy nods but chuckles, "Well, shit. You could hide a body back here pretty easily."

I stare at him. "That a common thing you see during inspections?"

"You'd be surprised, Tanner," he replies, exhaling deeply. "I have the most interesting job in the world here in Louisiana. You'd be shocked by what I've seen. But, I've been in the game long enough to not be surprised about anything more."

Thunder booms overhead.

He nods to himself. "I'll have the inspection report sent in, and y'all can get back to work Monday morning. You enjoy your weekend now."

"You too," I tell him, watching him walk away without so much as a glance back in my direction.

I make my way out to my crew just as the storm rolls over the top of the house. Everyone is gathering their tools.

"Just take your stuff home for the weekend," I tell them, nodding to the array of trucks and cars scattered around the driveway. "We'll start back up on Tuesday. I gotta get Jake here on Monday for a walk through before we start drywallin' this place up."

Jose sticks around while the rest of the crew leaves. I walk over to him, ignoring the lightning rippling overhead.

"Hey, I got a question," I say, and he straightens up, slugging his tool bag over his shoulder.

"Yeah, boss?"

"Were all the guys out here with you when Randy showed up?"

"Uh, yeah. We were all hanging out on the front porch."

"Everyone? Nobody was out back smoking?"

"No, I don't think so."

I nod, but an uncomfortable, twisting feeling settles in my gut. "All right. Take it easy this weekend. I'm gonna have you show up for a few hours on Monday while Jake's here. We need to have a plan going forward when it comes to doing the finish work, and you're the foreman for that."

"You got it, boss." Jose slaps me on the shoulder before walking out to his truck. I trust Jose. I've been working with him for years. He took over his dad's finish work company a few years ago, and I've kept him on as a contractor since then.

He's an expert in pretty much everything, so he's been here, at this job site, more than I have recently. If anything weird were going on, besides the problems with the tools, he'd know. And, more importantly, he'd tell me.

I get in my truck and leave the property, but as I get out to close the gate behind me at the very end of the driveway, I look back down the winding, cracked road. It's a tunnel, basically. Cypress trees hug either side, blocking out the sky.

It's so dark. So... endless. Like once you start driving down that driveway, you're driving into another realm entirely.

Just a few more months of this, I tell myself, and climb back into my truck.

When I get home, Bailey is waiting for me with a smile on her beautiful face and a hug that immediately makes me feel safe and comforted.

"How was the inspection?" she asks, resting her hands on my shoulders.

"We passed," I tell her, brushing my lips over hers. She tastes like chocolate and the diet sodas she likes so much. "Wanna go out to eat tonight?"

"You know I do," she smiles, leaning in as I kiss her fully. "Where?"

"Let's get out of Hahnville. I know a place in New Orleans you'll love."

"You really want to drive in this storm?"

"It's not that bad. I can handle a little rain."

# 7

# WHAT HAPPENED THERE?

Bailey

I SIP a cocktail in a quiet restaurant a few blocks away from Bourbon Street. It's a quiet Friday night because of the rain, but I don't mind.

Tanner leans back in his seat with an empty plate in front of him. That man can eat, that's for sure. No one has ever complimented my cooking like he does, and tonight he's already spoken to the chef of this little establishment twice, showering him with praise.

I smile at the thought and slide my leg against his under the table. He opens one eye and smiles softly at me.

"You look like you had a long day," I tell him.

He shrugs. "Yeah, well. It's been a long week. You've been gone, I've been splitting time between the job site and my shift at the firehouse."

"Well, we're home all weekend." I grin. "I think staying in bed until Monday is just what the doctor ordered."

"That sounds like heaven," he says, but his voice is wistful and withdrawn, like his mind is elsewhere.

I've known Tanner for a year. I've known him to be steadfast, stoic, and emotionally sound, but when I came home this morning after my night shift at the Wilsons', he seemed... off.

The memory of the other night when we slept together and he was... well... how do I describe it? I liked the sex. I really liked it, but Tanner and I have been sleeping together since a few days after we met, admittedly, and while he's always been generous, and I've been more than satisfied, his sudden shift threw me for a loop.

We've fallen into a routine. A kind of easy, mundane loop every day that feels safe, secure, and something I like. But something is different now. A new kind of energy ripples between us, and honestly, I've been a bit on edge.

I've chalked it up to working for the Wilsons and my increasing suspicions about how Robert got hurt, but it's been on my mind all week, and I really don't want to think about it anymore.

My phone buzzes in my purse, and I quickly glance at it, making sure it's not Helen needing my help tonight. Her sister is in town, as planned, to help on the weekend, but she's not a nurse.

"Oh, it's Layla," I smile, checking the text. "She's going to be coming here in a few weeks to visit. I guess she has to sign off on some paperwork with the historical society."

"It's probably because the new owners of the property want to drain and clear the marsh behind the backyard."

"Really?"

Tanner nods. "They want the cemetery out of there. I bet your friend has to sign off on allowing the bodies of her ancestors to be dug up and moved to lots at Hahnville Baptist."

I squirm. "I don't like that. That feels... wrong."

"I agree, but what can we do?"

I shrug, setting my phone on the table and resting my chin in my hand. "I think Layla will sign off on it. She seems more than ready to put that whole mess behind her."

But as I'm talking, Tanner straightens. His relaxed demeanor shifts, and the soft look in his eyes hardens, going dark around the edges.

Now I'm straightening up as a chill skitters down my spine. "Are you okay?"

"Why was Layla so willing to let go of that property? It's been in her family for over a century."

"She didn't feel any connection to it. Miss Penny was a distant cousin of hers, I guess. Not an aunt. Layla's family line wanted nothing to do with it, but Miss Penny made her the heir, and when she died, Layla and Dalton–"

"Dalton," Tanner says, low in his throat. It's an odd tone of voice that makes me narrow my eyes at him.

"You remember Dalton, right?"

"I haven't talked to him in a while," Tanner says, looking out the window at the rain. "Didn't know him well before that, either. I only know him as your friend's boyfriend."

"Okay... well, that's what he is. Yeah. Anyway, Layla wanted it to go to someone else, someone who actually wanted the property. When your client came in with an offer the first time, the historical society refused. I don't know why. But then they decided they couldn't do anything with it anyway. They wanted it when there was a house, but Penny leaving them a smoldering pile of rubble did nothing for the society. So they finally accepted the offer.."

"What happened to Layla there?" He says it in almost a whisper.

"Tanner, I don't really know. I've told you everything–"

"Tell me again." There's so much command laced through every word. It does something strange to my body. A mingled sense of desire and uncertainty wraps its way around my spine and tugs.

"She asked me often if the house was haunted. I said no, but looking back on it, I'm sure it was. She'd sense things in the house– see things. Then Vera started acting strange, and everything went downhill from there."

"How?"

"So many questions tonight," I try to tease, but he looks at me sharply. I sigh heavily. "What's wrong, Tanner? Is something going on over there?"

"You know about the power tools and all that mess. I just feel—feel uncomfortable there. Increasingly so. Like I'm being watched all the time."

I nod. It's all I can do, because the memory of the shadow I saw in the cemetery earlier this week flutters through my mind and forces me to suck in a breath.

"Do you think somebody's out there, in the marsh?" I ask quietly, reaching for his hand.

He allows me to curl my fingers around his thumb. I squeeze, and he seems to pop back to reality.

"Do I think someone is hiding out in the marsh?"

"It would explain all the weird things happening at your job site, right? The vandalism. I think—I think I saw someone out there the other night. I was out walking around Helen's property, trying to stay awake. I swore I saw someone standing in the middle of the grave-stones. And, you know, that's where Robert got hurt. What if someone is out there, and they hurt Robert, attacked him, and have been messing with your job site?"

"I doubt Robert got attacked. He's old, but not old enough to forget getting jumped—"

"I'm not sure he was meant to remember," I say as steadily as possible, trying to stay calm as I voice the inner turmoil that's been floating through my head all week while tending to his wounds. "I think whoever did this to him was trying to kill him, Tanner."

Tanner's eyes meet mine and hold my gaze for what feels like a very long time.

"I'm not sure I like you being at the Wilson house every night during the week."

I exhale deeply through my nose. "They need my help. It's not forever."

"Yeah, well," he sighs, leaning back and sliding his hand from mine. "I don't think anyone is in the marsh. I would've caught them by now. Someone on my crew would have seen them."

I nod and fall back into my own head as a waitress comes with the check. I don't even attempt to pull out my wallet because Tanner always pays, no expectations.

I'm trying to believe him. To believe, and to convince myself, that nothing is wrong, and the person I saw was only a trick of the mind–a mind exhausted by pulling a night shift for the first time in years.

But still, when we arrived back home forty-five minutes later, I feel... overwhelmed and a little scared.

I sit at the vanity Tanner built for me a few months after we started dating and slowly take off my earrings, my necklace, and the clip holding my hair away from my face. Through the mirror, I watch him sit on the edge of the bed and pull off his shoes and socks then his shirt.

I feel that tug again–that thing inside of me that's new and hungry.

He catches my gaze in the mirror and motions for me. "Come here, Bailey."

I stand on legs that don't feel like I have any control of them anymore and walk to him, slowly, wearing nothing but a camisole and the boy shorts I wore under the dress I had on during dinner tonight.

"What's wrong?" he whispers as I straddle his lap, wrapping my arms around his neck.

"I've just been... it's just been a weird week. A hard week."

"I know," he replies, brushing the words against my cheek as I close my eyes and let the world around us fade away.

His hands glide from my waist all the way up my back, and down again. It's a smooth, reassuring touch.

"Bailey," he says against my neck before kissing and sucking my skin. Through his jeans I can feel his hard cock twitch. I let out my breath, my heart skipping a beat as arousal surges through my body and settles in my core. "I'm going to fuck you," he rasps, dragging his teeth over my shoulder.

It's not a question. It's a promise. It's a command to obey, just like the other night when he folded me over the dining room table and took liberties with my body I'm not sure I would have allowed in any other circumstance or with anyone else.

But I don't expect him to flip me over. My back hits the bed, and then he's pulling his belt from the loops in his jeans and securing it tightly around my wrists before winding the rest of the length of leather around gaps in the headboard, tying it in place.

My wrists ache from how tight it is. I almost say something about the unwanted pain, but the words are stolen from my mouth as he unclasps his jeans and lets them fall to the floor along with his boxers.

His dick is hard as he crawls to me, kneeling above me, locking my legs in place beneath him. His eyes are dark, unreadable in the dimly lit room.

I gasp as he tears my camisole in half and roughly clutches my breasts. "Tanner–"

"Hush," he commands and leans down to kiss me.

I lose myself in his kiss, like usual. He is a drug, and I am desperate for anything I can get from him, but he pulls away briefly, reaching across the bed for his discarded jeans, and pulls out a pocket knife.

I hold my breath as the blade glides out and flashes in the fractured light coming from the lamp across the room.

I turn my heavy gaze from the knife to Tanner.

Am I scared or excited?

He holds my gaze as he lowers the blade and cuts through my boy shorts until I'm exposed to him.

He takes a deep breath, closing his eyes. I watch him curiously, noticing the way he seems to be... fighting something.

"Tanner," I whisper, wishing I could touch him right now, but my hands are bound, and I am completely at his mercy. "Tanner, are you okay?"

He blinks, his eyes remaining dark and hooded, and says nothing at all as he leans over my body and grips my thighs, wrenching them apart. The knife rests beside my head–so close I can see the raw blade in my peripheral vision.

The head of his cock splits me open, and he thrusts hard, sheathing himself in my pussy so deep I buck off the bed.

"Take it," he rasps against my neck, thrusting harder a second time, "Be a good girl, and take it all."

I choke out a moan as he grinds his hips against mine.

Whatever's gotten into him isn't a bad thing. I like it. Deep down, I want this. I want everything he can give me and more. It's like an obsession, like something dark and twisted that I've buried, and is now coming to life thanks to him.

But I close my eyes as my climax starts to roll through me, punctuated by each hard, deliberate thrust of his cock, and I feel like I might be passing out, because the edges of my vision go dark, and the man on top of me isn't Tanner anymore.

No, I'm... this isn't Tanner. This is–this is–

My scream echoes in my ears as the belt around my wrists is suddenly released, and Tanner is crushing my body against his. "Bailey? Bailey?"

I shove him away, rolling to the far edge of the bed and grabbing the pocket knife. My feet hit the floor, and I nearly topple over, my entire body numb and prickling back to life.

But I'm looking at Tanner. My Tanner. The man I've slept beside for a year. The man I know, inside and out... until recently.

I'm pointing his knife at him, and he's looking at me like he's just as confused as I am.

I drop the knife, my heart racing out of my chest.

"Bailey, what happened?" he asks, frantic. "You looked like you were passing out!"

"I don't know," I say hurriedly, stumbling back until my back hits the wall. I slide down onto my ass, and flinch away from him as he approaches me.

"Bailey, it's me–"

Somewhere outside the room, a song plays. The melody creeps into every air molecule and seeps into my brain like a virus. I've heard it before, but I can't place it.

"Where is that coming from?" I demand through tears.

"What are you talking about?"

"That song!"

"There's no song, Bailey."

8

—————————

## LET HER DIE

Tanner

I BARELY SLEPT last night or the night before. Bailey and I spent our weekend holed up in my house navigating a sudden rift that has formed in our relationship.

She barely looked in my direction all weekend. Even now, I can barely put into words what happened. One moment, we'd been having sex, and the next moment things got... hazy. Like I was standing outside of my body, watching, unable to stop the series of events unfolding in front of me as Bailey's eyes rolled back in her head and she was just... out. Out, for several seconds, then came to, screaming and pointing a knife at me.

I can't put my guilt into words, so I'm not going to even try. What's worse is the fact she spent the last two days trying to apologize to *me*.

It's safe to say my head isn't screwed on right today.

I step down off the foundation and onto the wide driveway at the old Gregory property and run my fingers through my hair before putting my cap back on.

Jose walks into view with his toolbox hoisted over one shoulder as the rest of the crew unload their tools from their trucks, ready to begin another week of work.

"I just got the inspection report, and we're green," I tell Jose as he steps up to my side. "I got the electricians and plumbers coming later this afternoon. You and the guys will be working around them until next Wednesday, and then we're starting sheetrock."

I spend the next twenty minutes explaining how today needs to go. This place needs to be spotless and prepared for the journeymen coming in to get this place hooked up to power and water.

This is the last phase of the heavy stuff, and in the next few weeks, we'll be moving on to finish work. Julia, the future lady of the house, has been blowing my phone all weekend with her cabinetry order for the kitchen and six bathrooms. All of the flooring, tile, and plaster has been ordered from Italy, of course, and is on its way.

A few weeks from now, I can cash in my final check and kiss this place goodbye.

Jose and the crew enter the skeleton-like depths of the house just as my phone rings, and I catch a glimpse of the caller ID before answering it right after the first ring.

It's the firehouse. Tyler, a volunteer firefighter, tells me there's a house fire on the outskirts of town in a subdivision full of brand new homes. It's electrical, by the sound of it.

It takes me a little under ten minutes to get to the neighborhood. My mind goes blank in that way only a situation like this can cause as I watch thick, black smoke funnel toward the cloudless sky.

The street is crawling with onlookers as I skid to a stop three houses down and sprint to the trucks, pulling on the gear I keep in my backseat in case of emergencies like this one.

"We got two units coming in from New Orleans, and an ambulance is on its way," Tyler shouts over the spray of water. The two-story new-build is entirely engulfed in flames, a total loss at this point, but the house to its left is burning now too. Its roof cracks, sending embers dancing down to the pristine, freshly landscaped front yard.

"How many people inside?" I ask before pulling on my helmet.

"None in that house, Johnnie got the neighbors on either side cleared out–"

"MY DAUGHTER!" A shrill scream cuts through the air, and I whirl as a young woman, no older than thirty, rushes toward the house with the roof fire.

One of my guys catches her around the waist before she even reaches the sidewalk. She screams again, and there's so much agony in her voice as she cries, "PLEASE! SHE WENT BACK INSIDE!"

Tyler and I look at each other before rushing to the distraught woman and find out she cleared out of her house with her three kids in tow, but her eight-year-old daughter slipped away. Her son, currently clutching her leg, mumbles something about a toy his sister didn't want to leave behind.

I'm putting on a mask before my brain catches up to the actions of my body. I pause, shouting to any firemen nearby, "Clear out the street, now!" I turn to the woman, shouting, "What is your daughter's name?"

"Rosie!"

The sirens from the two volunteer fire engines start a low, warning wail. The first house–where the fire originated–is about to collapse.

It's a hot, dry, windy day. The roof fire is spreading fast, and smoke is pouring from the windows.

There's a kid inside. The mother is beside herself as she sinks to her knees, begging for help.

I've been on the volunteer force for over a decade. Hahnville has never been big enough to justify having a paid fire department like New Orleans, and it takes too long for anyone from that city to get here in times like these.

I've gone into my fair share of fires to drag people out.

It's just another day at the office, as far as I'm concerned.

I turn and rush toward the house, kicking open the front door, and the air around me dissolves as acrid smoke fills the doorway.

The smoke rolls over me as I step inside. The house is already hot, and there's barely any breathing room. The sound of my own breath fills my ears. My gear is heavy, and the mask I'm wearing cuts into my skin as I pick my way through the lower level of the house, calling out Rosie's name.

Through the radio, I'm being told to hurry, to clear out. A tremor runs through the house as the neighboring home finally collapses.

It's far too fucking hot in here. Smoke rolls down the stairs as I head to the second level, kicking open doors, looking under beds.

*What's the point? It's just a little girl. What use is she? She'll just grow up to be as evil as the rest...*

I shake my head. Why would I think such a thing? It's like the thoughts invaded my mind, momentarily rendering me useless.

*Just let her die. You won't find her in time, anyway. She's probably already dead. Stupid little girl. She ran into the fire trying to find a toy. She wanted to die. Only someone who wants to die would run back into a burning building. Let her die. Let her die...*

I grunt with effort as I kick down the door in the upper floor hallway. What's wrong with me?

"Stop," I tell myself, but now I'm hesitating. A smoke-washed bathroom looms through the doorway I just kicked in.

It's the only room in the house I haven't cleared.

A voice in my radio tells me to fucking hurry, that I'm running out of time.

The ceiling is cracking with heat, the paint peeling as the walls start to smolder and the fire creeps from the attic to the second floor of the house.

*This place is a tinderbox, isn't it? I always said the new-build homes in this neighborhood weren't worth their asking price. Now look, some worthless kid is going to die. They'll put new homes on this lot. Maybe they'll build the houses better next time. Maybe her death was a good thing. Just let her die. Walk out, go home, take it out on Bailey. Wrap your hands around her slender neck and watch the life drain from her eyes...*

"ROSIE!" I shout into the bathroom. The house creaks and strains around me, dust drifting through the smoke as the fire eats into the second floor.

I step into the bathroom and pull back the curtain, finding the girl curled in the fetal position in the tub.

*Leave her. Leave her. Leave her.*

I feel like I'm fighting my own mind as I scoop her up and rush out of the bathroom. The second floor hallway is in flames, and I can't stop. The stairs start to crumble as I reach the last step and dart across the foyer, reaching the porch just as the fire licks down the stairs behind me.

I might be blacking out because I barely remember ending up in the front yard and the girl being lifted from my arms. I barely remember being dragged onto the road and my mask being yanked off my face.

I just remember the voice in my head telling me to let the girl die.

---

"I LOVE YOU. Goodnight. Try to sleep, okay?" Bailey's voice is a soft lullaby in my ear. I take a breath, my eyes fixed on the TV across the room.

"I'll try."

"They're saying you're a hero. They're right," she says softly, her voice echoing through the phone at my ear.

"I'll see you in the morning," I tell her, even though it's not true. She's at the Wilson's tonight, and I have to be at the job site at 6:00 A.M., but my mind isn't on Bailey or the fact we're going days without seeing each other right now.

In fact, that distance might be a good thing.

I watch images flee the fiery building in a flash across the TV screen. A reporter goes over the story–how the local volunteer fire department responded to a fire that ended up engulfing two homes, and seriously charring another. How the fire chief–me–rushed inside one of the burning homes to save the life of an eight-year-old girl, who is still in critical condition at a hospital in New Orleans.

They are, in fact, calling me a hero.

I suck down my second glass of whiskey as memories of the fire rush through my mind and blur my senses.

How could I have even thought about letting that kid die?

What's wrong with me?

*I could give you anything you wanted. Your darkest desires. Your wildest dreams.*

I stand on unsteady feet and walk into the kitchen to pour myself another drink.

*Tell me what you want, and it's yours. Money, fame. But not her. She's mine.*

I rub my ears and slam my hands on the counter. "What the fuck is wrong with you?" I ask myself through gritted teeth.

I feel like there's something crawling in my skull, trying to sink its talons into my flesh.

*I hate being ignored. This is for your own good. For her own good. Let me in, Tanner. Let me in and let's play my favorite game.*

I try to take a breath, but my chest is frozen. I feel light headed and woozy, and not from the alcohol blooming in my veins, no.

"Who are you?" I whisper to the empty room. "What do you want?"

# 9

## NIGHTMARE

Bailey

I'VE BEEN DISTRACTED all night, and it's no wonder. It was actually Helen who told me about the fire. I hadn't heard from Tanner all day, and suddenly Helen was dragging me into her living room where a video of Tanner bursting out of a burning building carrying an unconscious little girl was playing on a loop.

When I called him, he sounded distracted. I get it, of course. It takes a certain kind of person to run into danger and save a life. But still.... He sounded off, withdrawn, and so I've felt a little off kilter all night.

It's 4:00 A.M., and I'm sitting in the cramped office downstairs preparing my notes for Helen to take to Robert's doctor appointment later today. It's been a quiet night. Robert hasn't woken up a single time, and I've honestly just been twiddling my thumbs and trying to find something to do.

He starts physical therapy this week, and once he's back up on his feet enough to move around with the help of a walker, Helen wants me to switch to a day shift for the time being.

I'm looking forward to working during the daytime again.

I'm not cut out of long nights in dark, old houses.

But just as I'm finishing up my notes, I hear a thump upstairs.

I've grown accustomed to the pipes making noise at all hours of the night, but this was different. Something heavy just hit the ground, and after another thump sounds from above my head, I decide to investigate.

The door to the master bedroom is closed tight, but the door to the guest room is slightly ajar.

I hadn't left it open. I wonder if Helen came to check on Robert as I slowly push the door open, but Helen isn't in the room.

Robert, however, is out of bed and standing near the window.

"Robert!" I hiss, rushing forward. "You cannot be out of bed and putting pressure on your leg!"

He's a large man, and he swings an arm out, pointing a finger at me. "Don't touch me."

His cold tone works its way down my spine. I've never heard him use such a tone before—with anyone.

I look down at his leg. In the moonlight, I can see it shaking as he continues to put pressure on it.

"Please, at least sit down." I motion to the bed, but he isn't looking at me.

His eyes are fixed on something outside.

"Robert—"

"He's back. I knew he'd come back. *I knew* that fire wasn't enough to stop him."

"What—who are you talking about?"

"He's back. I knew it was him at those graves. Those graves gotta go. The whole marsh needs to burn to get rid of him—" he chokes on his words and looses a sharp, pained groan.

I grab him around the middle to steady him as he suddenly picks up his leg with a wince.

"Robert, I think you're dreaming," I say, tugging him toward the bed. "I think you're having a bad dream."

But he's much stronger than me, and he's working against me as I shove him toward the bed, which is only a few feet away from the window.

When I finally gain some ground, he grabs my shoulders, hard.

I gasp at the way his fingers are digging into my skin, but then he's shaking me like a ragdoll.

"DO NOT GO TO THAT HOUSE!" he bellows.

My ears ring as I try to pull away from him, but he continues to shake me hard enough my teeth clack together.

"Robert? ROBERT!" Helen's voice cuts through the sound of my teeth. She's at my side in an instant, prying Robert's hands from my body.

It takes a great effort for the two of us to get him back into bed, and even then, he's writhing and screaming and starting to babble incoherently.

"Do not let him out of bed!" I shout, then rush from the room, bounding down the steps to the office where I keep an assortment of supplies.

Robert's doctor prescribed some meds to help keep him calm. Thankfully, I have a liquid option and quickly fill a syringe before racing back upstairs.

Helen is pleading with Robert to calm down. He's covered in sweat, and I can see fresh blood pooling through his bandages where screws stick out of his skin.

I'm across the room in two seconds flat and stick in the needle in the meat of his upper arm.

Helen meets my eyes, her expression fearful and full of concern, but within moments, Robert starts to calm to the point he slips back into sleep.

Helen's lips part, but she can't find words to say. Neither can I, and we stand there in total silence for what feels like several minutes before she clears her throat and says, "I need a drink. It might be time to make a pot of coffee, don't you think?"

I nod, because it's all I can do, and follow her downstairs with the intent of gathering some first aid supplies to rebandage Robert's leg.

But she motions for me to follow her into the kitchen, and I do. I sit at the kitchen table, dropping the needle I need to properly dispose of, and run my hand over my face.

"The medication he's on for the pain can cause hallucinations in some people," I say robotically. "I organized my notes for his doctor. I'll mention tapering off those meds–"

"What was he saying to you before I came into the room?"

She starts the coffee maker and sits down across from me, her eyes glassy and still full of shock.

"He said not to go in that house. Was he talking about the old Gregory property?"

Helen doesn't answer. Her eyes on the floral tablecloth between us.

"Yeah. I think he might have had a nightmare about the night of the fire."

Again, I'm wondering if I was left in the dark about all of the details about the Gregory property, the family, and what led to the fire.

She gets up and pours two cups of coffee, mixing in a copious amount of sugar and cream. I take the cup she offers with gratitude as she sits back down.

"I'll talk to his doctor today and see what can be done."

"I'll fix up his leg before I leave–"

But Helen shakes her head, her eyes sliding to the rumpled fabric covering my shoulders–to the place where Robert had been clutching me for dear life, like he was worried I'd be ripped away from him by something unseen. "I'm not going back to sleep. You go ahead and head home, Bailey."

I leave the Wilsons' house twenty minutes later with a caffeine buzz and a lump in my throat. Weird things have been happening that I can't ignore. The bumps in the night are one thing, but seeing shadows, Robert acting like he's possessed, and the weird behavior and vague warnings from the Wilsons have me feeling on edge as I walk into Tanner's house and lock the door behind me.

He's at the firehouse tonight, so I'm alone, and the house is cool and quiet as I debate going back to bed right away or getting some work done.

I run a load of laundry and do some dishes. I mop the floors as the sun comes up. Around 8:00 A.M, I sit down at the dining room table with a fresh cup of coffee since I've already decided there's no way I can relax, not when my brain is telling me something is extremely wrong.

I pulled a knife on Tanner the other night. I thought–for a brief moment– I thought someone else had been in bed with me.

I toy with my phone before calling Layla.

It goes to voicemail.

"Hey, it's me. Look, I... I need to talk to you. It's about the night of the fire. Call me back."

I set my phone on the table just as Tanner walks through the door.

"Hey," he says, setting his duffle bag down. "I didn't think you'd be awake."

"I couldn't sleep. I didn't even try." I look down into my coffee.

Would Tanner think I'm crazy if I voiced what was going on in my head?

"Hey, uh... I wanted to talk to you about something," Tanner says. He leans against the archway leading out of the kitchen and crosses his arms.

He too looks like there's a lot on his mind that doesn't make sense, and I feel a smidge of the heaviness in my shoulder lift. I shift in my chair to face him. "Tanner, do you feel like... do you feel like something is going here, in Hahnville? Like, something is wrong, and you can't quite put a finger on it?"

Tanner holds my gaze and nods after a few seconds.

But we say, "You're going to think I'm crazy," in unison, and then stare at each other.

I start to stand, my heart beginning to race, but Tanner shakes his head. "I think you should sit down, Bailey."

10

―――――――――――

# SOMETHING'S NOT RIGHT

Tanner

THERE'S *something wrong with this place.*

The surety of the thought reverberates through my bones as I stand beneath the glare of the mid-morning sun, my eyes sweeping the hazy scene as though I'm seeing it all for the very first time.

"You okay, boss?" Jose's voice jolts me from the stupor I hadn't realized I'd fallen into. His tone is laced with concern and makes me wonder just how long I'd been staring off into the distance.

"I'm fine," I snap before wincing at my own gruffness. "Sorry," I add quickly. "Rough night."

Jose nods at my apology. "I figured as much. You're usually the first one here. It was weird being the only guy on site this morning. Honestly, this place gives me the fucking creeps."

"Tell me about it," I mutter.

My thoughts turn to yesterday's conversation with Bailey. It was a relief. I had let everything spill out, from the vandalism to the thoughts that didn't quite feel like my own. In turn, she told me about the figure she'd seen in the marsh and her rising unease about this place.

I promised her that I would wrap this project up as soon as I could. In a few more weeks, the house will be done, and I can pass off the fetid marsh and all of its ghosts onto the new owners. Let them deal with whatever haunts this damn swamp.

"Anyway," Jose continues, once again drawing me back to reality, "I had the guys start on installing the sheetrock this morning. They're making real good progress. Should be finishing up the kitchen and that little hallway soon."

"The hallway?" I repeat, realizing the implications.

"Yeah, why?"

"That's where those studs are, the ones we put too far apart. Not sure how we managed to leave that big gap in the wall. I was going to fix it this morning before y'all got here."

"Shit, boss, I didn't realize! They might not have gotten to that part yet."

"Don't worry about it," I huff, waving him away. "It's my fault for being late."

What's one more problem on this godforsaken site? I swear, this place is fucking cursed. The sooner we're done here, the better.

Frustration builds in me as I peel away from Jose's side and start toward the house. I hope they haven't gotten to that section of sheetrock yet. If they have, I'll have to tear that part down and redo the whole thing.

My anger doesn't mix well with the heat. It's still several hours before noon and the air is already moist and cloying. Sweat beads on my forehead. It's much too humid, and by the time I reach the front of the building, my shirt is clinging uncomfortably to my back. Though the swamp remains hidden by the hulking structure, the heavy stench of it curls through the shimmering heat. The scent is so strong that I can practically taste it with every breath I draw in.

It's as if the very air here is poison.

A shiver skitters down my spine despite the temperature. All at once, I feel the fine hairs on the back of my neck stand on end. Unseen eyes bore into the base of my skull, but when I turn, there's nobody in the driveway except for Jose, who's staring down at the screen of his cell phone.

"Get a fucking grip," I hiss to myself.

Steeling myself, I step into the house. My ears pick up the sounds of my crew talking and laughing over the sounds of power tools. I navigate easily through the maze of half-finished walls, following the ruckus until I find myself standing in the skeleton of what will soon be the kitchen and the short hallway right outside it that leads to a different living space.

"Boss," the nearest guy nods in greeting. He's got a sheet of drywall on a table and is measuring it with a measuring tape. Several of the other guys look up and acknowledge me in a similar manner.

Jose was right. They are doing good work, and the kitchen is almost completely finished. Unfortunately for me, they've done such a great job that they already fitted a sheet of drywall over the oddly spaced studs in the hall.

Inwardly, I curse. Outwardly, I thank the crew for their hard work and diligence. No use taking it out on them, not when they've already put up with so many missing tools and drained batteries. I'll take care of that section of framing later, I decide.

For a while, I get lost in my work. We finish the kitchen within the hour and move on to the dining room. There's no working AC or HVAC yet, and the manual labor has my muscles burning and sweat dripping down my brow. The air seems to grow heavier, and by the time we break for lunch in the early afternoon, it's evident that a storm's rolling in.

The rain holds off until the early evening. Bruise-colored clouds gather overhead and blot out the sun, though that does little to abate the heat of the day. As the rest of the crew packs up for the night, I return to the kitchen and start measuring the sheetrock I have to remove to get to the studs underneath to add the missing timber.

Just after I hear the last of the guys leave, the first peal of thunder booms in the distance. The whole foundation seems to reverberate with the rumble, and for one wild moment, I imagine the entire unfinished house caving in around me.

At that moment, a loud ringing noise erupts from the pocket of my jeans making me lose my breath.

I fish out my cell phone. The screen tells me it's Bailey calling. I answer midway through the third ring.

"Hey babe," I say.

"Hey," Bailey replies, her voice sounding oddly far away. I'm actually surprised I have enough bars to even hear her. Usually cell service doesn't carry this far, especially with a storm like this one.

"You okay?" I ask.

She's quiet for a moment, and then answers, "I guess. That was... a lot yesterday. I think I'm just really overwhelmed." I'm not sure what to say to that, so I wait until she speaks again. "I think we should leave town, Tanner."

"Leave?" I repeat. A tendril of dread blooms in the pit of my stomach. "We can't leave," I insist.

"Not permanently," Bailey backtracks. "Just for a night. Let's get a hotel room in the city on Saturday and hit the clubs. I just want us to get away from Hahnville for a bit, clear our heads. I need a distraction. Please?"

A frustrated sigh escapes my lips before I can stop myself. "I can't," I snap. "I have work to do here." I can almost picture the tears welling in her eyes as Bailey falls silent at my clipped tone. I sigh again, this time in shame. "Look babe, I'm sorry. I have to stay late to fix a fuckup today, and I just want get this whole job behind us."

"So you'll go?" she asks in a voice laced with hope.

"Sure," I say through gritted teeth. I can't deny her, not after I was so gruff with her. It might be a good thing to get out of town for a bit, to get away from this house. But then why did the thought of leaving make me feel sick to my stomach? "I'll book us a room," I assure her. "I love you."

"I love you too," she replies before ending the call.

I slip my phone back into my pocket and pick up the saw I'll use to cut into the sheetrock. Around me, the house settles against the storm. Sheets of rain tear down from the skies, pummeling the roof in a way that sounds almost like footsteps.

As lightning flashes, I hear another sound struggling for dominance against the roiling of the storm. For a moment I think it's somebody talking, but then I realize it's singing.

*Folks, I'm goin' down to St. James Infirmary...*

I strain to hear the next line, but it's lost in a peal of thunder.

"What the fuck?" I mutter as I put the saw down on the table and head toward the sound.

*She'll never find another sweet man like me....*

I track it through a few rooms, but the melody seems just out of reach. Finally, I find myself at the back door of the house, squinting through the portal into the back yard. The grass here was singed in the fire and never bounced back, but the marsh remained untouched.

"Who's there?" I call into the darkness, but the rain sweeps my voice away.

*When I die, bury me in my straight-leg britches...*

Bailey mentioned that she thought somebody might be living in the swamp. Could she be right? Even as I struggle to see through the rain and the fading light, I swear I can see a figure standing among the graves of the sinking cemetery.

"Hey!" I shout. "You're trespassing!"

The figure doesn't move.

Anger surges through me. Whoever, or whatever, this is, this thing has been terrorizing my girl, my crew, and me. A wave of adrenaline propels me forward, and I rush out into the rain.

I'm across the dead lawn in seconds, and before I realize it, I'm knee deep in the thick soup of the swamp. Rancid water oozes into my work boots as I drag myself through the muck toward the gravestones.

The figure waits, watching me struggle against the sludge. It feels like an eternity passes before I finally make it to the edge of the cemetery. I'm out of breath and covered in mud, but I'm ready to swing at whoever this is. I'm close enough that I can tell it's a man, but it's too dark and rainy to see much more than that.

"Who the fuck are you?" I demand, my voice barely audible over the storm.

The figure cocks his head but doesn't reply.

I storm over to him and reach out to grab his arm, but as soon as my hand makes contact with what should be solid flesh, the figure dissolves in my grasp in a torrent of putrid mud. The ooze splashes down around me with a sickening slurp.

For a moment, I stand there in pure shock.

Then the fear kicks in, and before I can even make a conscious decision, my feet are carrying me back the way I came. In a daze, I clear the marsh and stumble across the lawn toward the back door.

"What the fuck? What the fuck?" I chant as I fling myself inside the structure. "What the fuck was that?"

I don't stop until I reach the kitchen and the safety of the work lights. Gasping for breath, I collapse against the doorframe.

I think for a moment that I'm okay now. Everything in here is familiar, just how I left it.

But then dread floods through me once again as I scan the room. My eyes catch on the far wall, which should be covered in fresh sheetrock.

The section over the misplaced studs is destroyed. It's just a mess of jagged edges and dusty fragments now. It's as though something had been enraged and clawed into it.

Or maybe something clawed its way out.

Either way, I'm not going to stay to find out.

# 11

# CAN'T GET AWAY

Bailey

HAHNVILLE IS in the rearview mirror, literally.

I blow out a sigh of relief as the last exit sign for the town fades into the distance behind us. The bustle and lights of NOLA beckon, and I let myself relax more with every mile we cover. A shadow has plagued us the last few weeks. I can't deny that any longer, just as I can't deny that I can feel its noxious grip on me loosen as we put more distance between us and the marsh.

"I can't wait to show you the club," I gush. "The DJ tonight is supposed to be great. I plan on dancing the night away!"

My enthusiasm is contagious, and Tanner stands no chance against it. "Oh?" he asks, smirking playfully. "What kind of dancing can I expect tonight? Grinding? Twerking?" He waggles his eyebrows suggestively and I giggle.

"The funky chicken," I reply in the driest tone I can muster.

Tanner lets out a booming laugh, and I quickly join him. Somewhere in the back of my mind, I realize that I haven't heard him let loose like that in quite some time. I dimly recognize that I should be concerned about that, but I'm too caught up in savoring the moment to dwell on it.

The rest of the drive passes quickly. We joke around, and I even manage to coax another chuckle out of Tanner. The sound zings straight to my core, reminding me that we haven't had sex for a while either. The promise of the hotel room at the end of the night becomes almost as enticing as my man's laugh, and I find myself squeezing my thighs together until we pull up in front of the club.

It takes us a few minutes to find parking, but Tanner manages to ease his oversized truck into one of the tiny spaces along the busy street. I never knew that a man parallel parking could be so sexy.

"Ready?" he asks as he joins me on the sidewalk outside the club.

I pause for a moment to admire the handsome angles of his face, his tanned skin, the roots of stubble freckling his jaw. He's gorgeous, and he's mine. I flash him a saucy grin and loop my arm through his. "Always," I answer, slightly breathless.

We have no problem getting into the club. The bouncer simply squints at our IDs and steps aside to let us in.

The atmosphere transforms the moment we cross the threshold. Bass throbs, igniting the fire inside of me that's been smoldering since Tanner laughed in the car. I close my eyes and breathe deeply. Sweet alcohol and perfume invade my nose, a far cry from the fetid odor of the marsh. Bodies writhe in every corner, chasing out any of the ghosts of Bourbon Street that might have a mind to linger. This place is alive in the same way the swamp is dead.

I reach down and take Tanner's hand and squeeze. He returns the pressure, smiling down at me. I'm sure now that this was a good idea, that all we needed was to get out from under the shadow of the Gregory place.

Tanner tugs me by our linked hands, guiding us through the throng of bodies towards a free table near the back of the club. I slide into one of the high-top seats, but he doesn't sit.

"Stay here," Tanner orders, his hot breath caressing the shell of my ear. "I'll get us some drinks."

The heat of his body sweeps away as he weaves towards the bar, and I shiver at the sudden loss. I pull out my cell phone and scroll through my socials as I wait for him, but my mind is too busy thinking about all of the other things he'll order me to do tonight to pay much attention to the screen, and I end up sliding the device back into my purse only a few seconds later.

By the time Tanner returns, I'm properly hot and bothered. I barely even notice that his hands are empty. In that moment, I can think of far better things those fingers could be doing.

"Let's dance," I say. It's more of a command than a suggestion, and he doesn't look like he's about to argue.

I once again take him by the hand and lead him to the dance floor. The space is already crowded, but I zero in on a spot closer to the door, and we quickly claim it as our own.

Our movements start out innocently enough. I wrap my arms around Tanner's neck. He's so tall I have to stand on my toes to reach. He splays his hands on my hips and then roughly pulls me forward so that our bodies meet in the middle, resulting in a delicious lack of negative space between us. The lights pulse around us, disorienting me in the best way. I haven't even had a sip of alcohol yet, but the heartbeat of the music gives me a heady feeling like I've already had several shots.

A serene smile slips across my face as I let my eyelids flutter closed. I've always loved dancing. My career as a nurse has often forced me to be serious and to consider other people's needs before my own. But with music like this sultry fusion of jazz and techno, I can let everybody else go and focus solely on myself. Dancing is like sex to me, but the pleasure is solely mine.

I let the pulsing beat guide my moves, the music feeding into my limbs as I slide against the hard planes of Tanner's body. I can feel how much he's enjoying this through his jeans. The friction is maddening, and I decide that tonight, I want to lose my fucking mind.

As if sensing my thoughts, Tanner flips me around suddenly so that my back molds to the front of him. His hardening cock presses against me through constraining layers of fabric. Lust ricochets through my veins as I grind onto him in time with the music, teasing him with my curves. His large hands begin to roam, sliding up my sides and brushing the edges of my breasts. A pulse of pleasure thrums through me at the contact, but it's not enough.

"More," I urge, though realistically I know that there's no way he can hear me over the driving beat of the music. Even so, he seems to come to the same conclusion. He leans over, his body crushing fully against mine as we sway to the bass, and he catches the shell of my ear with his teeth.

I gasp at the contact and arch back against him. "More," I repeat. I need more. I need *him.*

His mouth hovers just over the spot he bit. "Beg," he commands, his voice low and gravelly. "Beg me for it."

I nearly come undone at his words. All I can do is pant, "Please, Tanner. Please."

He leans down further and chuckles against the crook of my neck. I turn my head to grant him better access, and he immediately latches onto my pulse point, sucking and licking as he continues to grind his hips into mine.

"More," I urge. "Please, I need more."

A whimper escapes my lips as his hands course down my body. One wraps one around my waist, holding me to him in a vice grip. The other snakes beneath the short hem of my dress, trailing fire in its wake.

"Is this what you want?" he murmurs in my ear. "Do you want me to touch you?"

"Please," I gasp as his mouth returns to my neck.

Before I even have time to form a coherent thought, he pulls the edge of my lacy thong aside and runs one thick finger through my slit.

I jump at the sudden contact, but his arm clamps around me, holding me in place. I melt into him as he once again rubs his finger against my slick heat before pushing roughly inside me. I groan in pleasure as he works in a second finger before pulling out, only to curl them back in at precisely the right angle to have me seeing stars.

"Fuck," I moan, my head rolling back against his chest as he pumps his fingers in and out of my pussy. I can feel my own wetness trailing down my thighs as he brings me higher in rhythm to the pounding of the base.

"Do you like that?" he asks in a voice like black velvet. I'm dimly aware that his tone sounds off somehow, but I'm far too distracted to care. "Look how wet you are for me. Are you so much of a slut that it turns you on that I'm fucking your tight little cunt with my fingers in front of all these people?"

I blink, fighting against the haze.

Something about this is wrong. Tanner's never spoken to me like that, not even in our kinkiest moments. He's never degraded me or talked down to me like this. I try to pull away, but his arm cages me in, tightening around me so much that it starts to hurt. The pleasure begins to fade as reality sinks in.

"What's the matter, Bailey?" His voice is more a hiss than a purr now in my ear. "Don't you want everybody to see you come on my fingers like the dirty little whore that you are?"

As he speaks, his voice changes, and all at once I realize that whoever is behind me is *not* Tanner.

Panic flares through me, flooding my veins and imbuing me with the strength to move. I struggle against him, flailing my arms and twisting my body until I'm able to wrench free of his grasp. His fingers slip from inside of me as his grip around my middle breaks. I push away from him and then spin to face him, my hand raised and ready to slap him square in the face.

But shock strangles me as I stare up at the man who had touched me.

"Dalton?" I gasp.

The man in front of me is still for a moment. Under the shifting lights of the club, he sure looks like Layla's boyfriend. The angles of his face and the color of his hair match. But then one of the lights hits him just right, and I realize that his eyes are black, not the jade green that they should be.

This is not Tanner, and it's definitely not Dalton either.

I don't think he's even a person.

It grins at me, and it's like watching a corpse with rigor mortis try to smile.

Every atom in my body screams at me to run, and that's exactly what I do. I stumble, reeling backward into the sea of bodies, fighting against the current. I don't even know where I'm going. All that matters is that I get away from that thing, as far away as possible.

Out of nowhere, two strong arms grab me and spin me around. I struggle for a moment before a familiar, concerned voice asks, "Bailey? What's wrong babe?"

"Tanner?" I ask weakly.

"It's me," he nods, confusion wrapping around his features. And in that moment, I'm sure that this is the real Tanner. "What happened, Bailey?" he asks gently. "You look like you've seen a ghost."

"That man," I manage, turning to point to the thing that looked like Dalton.

But when I look, the thing is gone, as though it was never even there at all.

12

———————

## HUNTED

Tanner

BAILEY IS CRYING.

My hands tighten on the steering wheel as I try to tamp down my anger at whoever touched my girl. She had been borderline hysterical in the club and had insisted that I take her home. All plans of a romantic night at a NOLA hotel have vanished, and now we're retracing our steps back to Hahnville.

I glance over at Bailey, who's curled up in the passenger seat. "You okay?" I ask for probably the hundredth time.

"I'm fine," she responds faintly. We both know that's a lie, but I don't call her on it. "I'm sorry I ruined our night."

"You didn't ruin anything," I tell her firmly. "That guy should never have fucking touched you. You didn't do anything wrong. He did."

She doesn't reply. She simply turns her head to the window, her eyes straying to the glass and the darkness beyond.

Mirroring her, I fix my gaze on the road ahead. There aren't many cars out on the highway this late, so we're making good time. My mind drifts to earlier, when we first left Hahnville. Everything had felt so wrong on the drive out, like something terrible would happen if we didn't stay.

And then something bad *had* happened, even though I don't fully understand what Bailey experienced in the club.

I can't shake the nagging feeling that whatever's haunting us is angry that we tried to get away. Maybe it will be safer to stay in Hahnville, to ride this thing out until the house is done, and Bailey's stint as Robert's night nurse wraps up. Anxiety blossoms in the pit of my stomach as I wonder if there even is a way out for us. Surely, this thing can't hunt us forever?

Neither of us speaks again until we pull into the driveway.

"I'm sorry," Bailey murmurs again, her soft voice slicing through the oppressive silence that has settled between us. Her soulful eyes are red from crying, and the sight sends a pang of protectiveness rushing through me. I take her small hand in one of mine.

"You have nothing to apologize for," I insist, lifting her palm to my lips and kissing it gently.

She shakes her head, fresh tears brimming in her eyes. "I just...I feel like we're being toyed with, like it's trying to drive us crazy," she whispers.

I weave my fingers between hers and squeeze gently. "Whatever is going on, we won't let it come between us," I reassure her, injecting as much confidence as I can muster into my tone. "We're stronger than this. If there are any ghosts in that old swamp, they aren't tearing us apart."

Bailey closes her eyes and draws in a shaky breath. "You really mean that?" she asks.

"I sure do." I sound so certain, but underneath, a thread of doubt weaves its way between my bones.

When she opens her eyes again, she's gazing at me with such intensity that my heart stutters in my chest, though that doesn't seem to stop the blood from pumping downward.

"Show me." Her words are somewhere between a plea and a command. "Show me that you mean it."

And so I do.

There is nothing gentle in the way I capture her mouth with mine. She moans against me, and I take the opportunity to taste her, darting my tongue between her swollen lips. I pour every ounce of feeling into the kiss, willing her to feel just how much I fucking love her.

Bailey responds in kind. Her hands catch the collar of my shirt, and she draws me closer, deeper. Desire blossoms off her, infecting me with its heady promises as her fingers trail downward toward the visible bulge in my jeans.

"Fuck," I groan as she palms my cock through the thick material, sending sparks of pleasure ricocheting through my veins.

Bailey pulls back a little, her gaze fixed hungrily on the fly of my jeans as she eases the zipper down. The thin glow of the streetlight filters into the darkened cab through the windshield, and when it catches her face, she looks otherworldly, like an angel fallen to earth. She's the most beautiful creature I've ever seen.

Her hand closes around my cock, and I nearly come right then and there.

Nimble fingers ease over my shaft as Bailey finds a slow, agonizing rhythm. My head falls back against the headrest. I'm lost to the electric heat of it.

Just when I think it can't get any better, Bailey shifts, and then her tongue swipes the head of my cock, teasing me.

"Don't start something unless you're prepared to finish it," I growl in warning.

"I wouldn't dream of it." She smirks.

Before I can respond, her mouth closes around my cock.

I don't make any effort to stifle my groans. My hands thread through her hair, guiding her into a quickening rhythm as I thrust my hips up to meet her. Somewhere in the back of my mind, I worry that

I'm being too rough with her, but that thought evaporates as I feel myself nearing my limit.

I stop her then, shuddering from the effort.

"You're mine," I growl down at her. "You're mine to protect, mine to love."

"I'm yours," she confirms breathlessly.

God, she's so fucking gorgeous like this, with her mussed hair and swollen lips.

"Let's get inside," I say, and she nods eagerly. There are so many things I'm going to do to her tonight, but I'd rather not fuck my girl senseless in front of any nosy neighbors.

I intended to take her straight to the bedroom, but we don't make it that far. Instead, as soon as the door closes, I pin her to it, her body molding to mine as I steal another kiss from her.

My cock, tucked back in my jeans, twitches between us. Bailey, eager for more friction, wraps her legs around me and lets out a moan as I rock my hips into hers. Caging her in with one arm, I trail the other hand down until I reach the thin fabric of her panties.

"You're so fucking wet for me," I murmur in her ear as I ghost my fingers over her dripping pussy. "You're going to feel so good around my cock."

Bailey moans again. The needy sound has me catching the thin straps of her dress with my index fingers. I yank the top down, exposing her full breasts to the sultry night air. Her nipples are peaked with desire, and I can't help but lean down to capture one between my teeth.

We stay like that for a moment, Bailey writhing against me as I tease her. Finally, she pushes me back, hard enough to make me stumble. I'm confused for a split second until she plants her hands on my chest and forces me toward the bedroom, and I understand what she wants.

She pushes me back onto the bed, and I let it happen. I'm intrigued. Sure, Bailey's initiated sex before, but never like this. The way she stares down at me, like a predator surveying its prey, is new and sends a delicious shiver down my spine.

My eyes are hooded with desire as I watch her once again free my cock from the confines of my jeans. I expect her to take me in her mouth again, but instead, she crawls up me until I can feel the wetness of her panties against my shaft.

Bailey rocks against me, and I groan as the friction once again starts to build. At the same time, her fingers work feverishly to undo the buttons of my shirt. After a few fruitless seconds, she simply grabs the fabric and tugs sharply, sending buttons flying.

It's the hottest thing I've ever seen.

I quickly change my mind, however, when she pulls her panties to the side and positions herself over my straining cock.

"Fuck," I groan as she sinks down onto my shaft. Her wet heat sets my blood on fire, and I buck my hips up hard, unable to stop myself.

A lurid moan slips from her lips. "Tanner," she breathes, her blazing eyes meeting mine. Her hands find purchase on my chest as she lifts her hips until I'm almost fully unsheathed. In the next breath, she slides back down, impaling herself on my cock.

The feel of her pussy around me sends me into a frenzy. I thrust up into her, meeting her rhythm as she writhes above me.

Moonlight halos her as she loses herself in her pleasure. Her messy hair cascades down her back, and her cinnamon skin seems to glow in the darkness. My eyes hungrily skim the peaks of her breasts as they bounce with each thrust, the arch of her back, the graceful curve of her neck.

She's fucking perfect.

It doesn't take long for the pressure to coil inside of me. I feel myself getting closer, but I want Bailey to come first. I can tell by the feel of her that she's nearly there, ready to unravel.

With one last thrust, she topples over the edge, clawing at my chest as she shatters above me.

Her pussy spasms around my cock, pushing me to my own

blinding release. I empty myself inside her with one last buck of my hips as she chants my name over and over again like a prayer.

Utterly spent, Bailey collapses down onto my chest. I pepper her brow with soft kisses, savoring the weight of her.

"I love you," I whisper to her in the moonlit dark. "I really fucking love you."

It's only when she doesn't answer that I realize she's fallen asleep.

I stay with her for a while just listening to the steady sound of her breathing. It's grounding. It tells me she's here, and she's okay. Whatever is happening, we'll be okay.

Finally, my bladder convinces me that I need to get up. I shift Bailey as gently as I can and tuck the blankets in around her. She barely stirs. That's a good thing. She's been so tired lately after working those damn night shifts. She'll feel better tomorrow after a solid night of sleep.

I make my way to the bathroom and close the door before turning on the light. Squinting against the sudden brightness, I catch a glimpse of myself in the mirror.

"Holy shit," I mutter as my eyes adjust. My chest is crisscrossed with a series of deep red scratches. I vaguely recall the scrape of Bailey's nails against my chest as she came, but I didn't realize she had been quite so vicious.

This isn't like the sweet and kind Bailey I know at all. But the red marks on my chest are hard to argue with.

*What if she does worse next time?*

I blink.

Why would I think something like that?

My eyes hover over the scratches in the mirror and then wander up to my face.

Ice thrills down my spine as I realize that the visage I'm looking at is not my own.

For a moment, I have the absurd thought that it's Dalton, Layla's boyfriend. But the face is wrong somehow, like it has been poorly rendered in wax from somebody's memory. Whatever it is, it's grinning madly, and it's certainly not a man.

A peal of thunder rolls in the distance, causing me to jump. The subsequent flash of lightning has my eyes darting to the window before returning to the mirror.

The thing that isn't Dalton is gone.

My own face stares back at me, horror alight in my eyes.

And when the next roll of thunder rattles Hahnville, I swear it sounds like laughter on the wind.

# 13

## SWAMP

Bailey

SOMETHING SINISTER IS WATCHING me from across the swamp.

I stand in the window of Robert's bedroom, squinting out into the oppressive darkness, but there's nothing much for me to see. The emergent structure of the nearly finished house juts out over the tops of the cypress trees like the horns of some monstrous beast. Beyond, the swamp lies swathed in humid shadow, as still and silent as the graves that sink ever deeper into the putrid muck.

Whatever waits for me in the marsh, it doesn't show itself. Not tonight, at least.

I shiver and draw the blinds, blotting out the night beyond the window.

Beside me, Robert doesn't stir. He's been asleep for about half an hour now after receiving another dose of pain medication. Hopefully, he'll slumber through the night. I've already cleaned and bandaged his wound, so there's not much for me to do now other than check in on him periodically. I decide to head downstairs to the kitchen and make a cup of coffee to help keep me awake throughout the remainder of my shift.

With gentle footsteps, I cross the room and slip out into the hallway beyond. Helen's left the landing light on for me, and I'm grateful that I don't have to feel my way downstairs in the dark.

I make my way down quickly, darting through pools of shadow as I go. It feels like I'm a kid again, like I'm running from half-believed monsters reaching for me in the darkness. By the time I step into the warm light of the kitchen, my heart is hammering in my chest as though I've run a marathon. Though I know it's silly, I glance over my shoulder into the inky blackness of the first floor, just in case something really is nipping at my heels.

There's nothing there, of course.

I blow out a shaky breath. I feel foolish for being so on edge, but if I'm entirely honest with myself, I've been off kilter since Tanner and I went on our failed trip into town over the weekend.

The fine hairs on the back of my neck prickle to life as I recall the unfamiliar hands that had roamed my body in the club. At the time, I had thought that the thing had looked like Layla's boyfriend Dalton, but now I wonder how I could have ever drawn that comparison. It had been so wrong, so *other*. How could I have ever thought it was human?

The worst part wasn't even how the thing had violated me. No, it's how I acted after that really scares me. I was so frightened that I'd clung to Tanner with strength I barely even recognized. The next morning, I was horrified to see that I'd marred his sculpted chest with long red scratches, deep enough to draw blood. Tanner insisted that it was fine, but he had been acting so strangely since then.

Had I done more than just hurt him physically?

"Stop it," I whisper out loud to myself. There's no use in jumping down that rabbit hole again. I decide to bring it up to Tanner first thing tomorrow morning before he leaves for the construction site, and my mind quiets a little in the face of my resolve.

Moving on autopilot, I kick myself into gear and start the process of putting on the coffee. Soon enough, the kitchen is filled with the gurgling hum of the percolator. It's a comforting sound, just loud enough to drown out the coiled silence of the night without waking the couple sleeping upstairs.

Once the coffee is done, I pour myself a cup and then settle at the broad kitchen table to read. I'm halfway through a romance novel, one of those British regency ones where everybody wears elaborate dresses and drinks tea with chaperones. As I lose myself in the tapestry of letters, I can't help but picture Tanner as the dashing male lead. I bet he'd look delicious in one of those high-collared jackets and an ascot.

*Thump.*

A soft sound on the stairs jolts me from my drifting thoughts.

All at once, my heart strains against my ribs in a frantic tattoo. I sit rigidly in my chair, spine taught as ice curls down my vertebrae. My eyes strain to see something, anything, moving in the darkness beyond the kitchen doorway.

And then relief washes through me as Helen steps into the light.

I exhale loudly, my body sagging back into the chair.

"Oh, honey! Did I scare you?" Helen fusses, bustling over to give me a soothing half-hug. "I'm so sorry, I didn't mean to sneak up on you."

"It's fine," I say, though my voice shakes a bit from the sudden rush of adrenaline.

The older woman pulls back to regard me and frowns. I know I have dark circles under my eyes that my foundation doesn't quite cover. "Have you been sleeping, honey? I'd hate to think these night shifts are taking a toll on you," she chides.

I shake my head. "I'm just a little jumpy, that's all."

Helen's frown deepens. I don't miss how her eyes flicker toward the window overlooking the backyard and the swamp beyond before her gaze returns to me. "Is everything okay?" she asks, her voice low as though she's worried somebody, or something, might be listening.

For a moment, I consider telling her about what's happened, but how am I supposed to explain it to somebody as practical and reasonable as Helen?

My pause is too long. I half expect Helen to push, but instead, she points at the mug still clutched in my hands and asks, "Is there enough for two?"

"Sure," I nod, relieved that she seems to have dropped the subject.

The night seems clearer now that Helen is here with me. I watch her as she retrieves a mug from the cupboard and pours herself a generous helping of caffeine. Her movements are sure and familiar, reminding me of my mom.

Once her coffee is prepared, Helen settles into the chair beside me. For a moment, we're silent against the nightly backdrop of humming insects and the wind murmuring through the gnarled branches of the cypress trees.

Finally, Helen speaks. "How was your weekend away?" she asks. I sense that there are other questions brewing beneath the surface of her words, but I choose to answer only the one put in front of me.

"It was fine," I reply in what I hope is a cheerful tone.

Helen raises an eyebrow and takes a sip from her mug. "Just 'fine'?" she prods. "You're telling me that that handsome man of yours took you to a fancy hotel in town for the weekend, and it was just 'fine'?"

Normally, I probably would've blushed at the older woman's insinuation, but now I just shrug. "We had a good time," I lie.

It's clear that Helen is not convinced. "Is something going on with you and Tanner?" she inquires. "Are you two fighting? Or are you..." Her voice trails off, but she completes the thought by gesturing to her stomach.

"No, nothing like that!" I squawk, my cheeks reddening. "We're just...going through a rough patch, is all."

"He's not hitting you, is he?"

"Absolutely not!" The question raises my defenses, but I don't want to snap at Helen like that, not when she's only looking out for me. "I'm sorry," I apologize meekly. "Tanner's a good man, he'd never do anything to hurt me. He's just been so busy at the old Gregory place. I think it's taking a toll on both of us."

Concern flashes across Helen's features. "Have you been spending much time out there?" she asks. It's an innocent enough question, but her words are laced together with worry, and I can't help but wonder if she's ever seen shadows shifting out there late at night.

I shake my head, hopefully assuaging her fears. "I haven't been back since the fire," I say. "Tanner doesn't want me anywhere near there. He says that all it'll take is one good flood and the swamp will swallow that house up whole."

"He's right, you know," Helen sighs, relief evident in her tone. "He must be almost finished by now."

"Just a little bit longer," I confirm.

We fall silent once again. Questions roll through my mind, but I have no idea how to pose any of them without Helen thinking I'm a few cards short of a deck. After a long moment, I finally decide on a safe bet and ask, "Have you talked to Layla recently?"

Helen's eyebrows shoot up. "No," she replies. "Why?"

I hesitate for a second before blurting out, "I thought I saw Dalton."

Alarm storms through Helen's eyes. "Dalton? Layla's boyfriend? You're sure?"

"Yeah, I thought I saw him at the club," I explain. "But I don't know if it was him. It was... weird." It's the understatement of the year, but I don't know how else to frame it in a way that doesn't make me sound like I've lost my mind.

"Maybe you should call Layla," Helen suggests. "I'm sure she can help."

I nod along. "I owe her a chat anyway."

But really, I don't know what I would say to Layla if I called. Hey, your boyfriend, who looked really demonic for some reason, did unspeakable things to me in a club? Best case, it really was Dalton, and it would only cause Layla pain to know what he had done. Worst case, I would be dragging Layla back into the nightmare she had survived in her tenure as Penny's night nurse.

Layla had never actually told me much of what had happened at the old Gregory place. I knew that it was bad, and that Dalton had saved her somehow, but she hadn't ever said much more than that, and I hadn't pushed. And she seems so happy in Florida, away from the shadows of the swamp. Could I really shatter her peace like that?

No, I decide. I'll leave it alone.

Helen stays in the kitchen for a bit longer, and I'm grateful for her company. But after a while, the night overtakes her, and she retires upstairs with a yawned goodnight.

Once the house is quiet again, I get up and wander to the windows that overlook the backyard. The swamp stares back at me, festering in the humid darkness.

Inevitably, my focus drifts back toward the cemetery and the unfinished building that peers over the tops of the cypress trees. The newly installed windows gaze back with matte eyes, and I shiver.

The place is terrible in the dark. But I know that under the harsh summer sun, the shadows shrink back, and the ghosts that reside there have nowhere to hide.

I'll go there tomorrow morning, I decide. I'll face that wretched house in the burning light of day and curse out whatever skulks there.

It's only a house, I tell myself.

It's only a house.

14

______________

## ALL FALL DOWN

Tanner


I DON'T BELIEVE in ghosts.

At least, that's what I tell myself as I linger in the backyard of the old Gregory place. The swamp stretches out before me, the ancient cypress trees cloaked in green haze beneath the overcast sky. From where I stand with the house rearing up behind me, I can almost taste the fetid stench of the mire. It's the smell of decay and rotting things, a primal scent that sets my nerves on fire.

It reeks of danger and death.

But is there something more out there, lurking amidst the sunken tombstones? My mind drifts back to the figure I followed into the swamp and the face I saw in the mirror, and I have my answer.

"Stay the fuck away from us," I mutter. Even though my voice is low, I have a feeling that the thing in the marsh will hear me anyway.

I turn away then and traverse across the brittle lawn back toward the house.

The structure is very nearly finished. The new materials of the exterior are pristine, though I know that nature will render them dull and mossy with time. Clear windows line the walls, a dozen vacant eyes staring emptily into the swamp. The sounds of power tools and chatter drift out through the open ones, and I can hear a radio playing somewhere deep in the belly of the beast. On the surface, it seems like just another normal job.

So why do I have the terrible sense that something evil is about to happen?

Maybe it's because of the argument Bailey and I had this morning. Although we've had our fair share of disagreements throughout our relationship, this was the first time we had ever really fought.

Bailey asked to come to the job site with me this morning. I said no. It should've been case closed.

And yet, Bailey pushed back. I've always admired her for her stubbornness and perseverance, but this was the first time it had been turned on me.

"Why not?" she asked, her hands on her hips and a challenge in her tone.

"You know why," I responded. "It's not safe, not with that thing out there."

"Maybe we have to face it," she argued.

I rolled my eyes then. "I don't think this is the sort of thing that'll just leave us be if we ask it nicely."

"Well, we have to try something," she insisted. "Do you really just want to sit here and wait for it to fuck with us again?"

I shrugged in response. "I'd rather you stay as far away from that house as possible."

"While you go to work there every day?"

"That's different," I protested.

"How? How is that any different?" she threw back at me.

The argument went in circles from there until frustrations on both sides reached a boiling point. I raised my voice to her, and was shocked to see tears welling in Bailey's eyes.

"I'm going out," she said, grabbing her purse and slamming the door behind her. I had no idea where she went, and she hasn't responded to any of my texts since.

I didn't mean to snap at her like that. It was as though my mind had been stacked with kindling. The spark of our argument flared until the flame was raging out of control, an inferno of emotion. I can't even remember the last time I was that angry.

Shame surges through me as I step through the back door and into the relative coolness of the house.

"You okay, boss?" Jose asks, peering up at me from where he's crouched near a baseboard working on installing some molding.

"Yeah," I reply gruffly. "Where are we at?"

Jose glances over his shoulder. "The guys are papering the bedrooms upstairs, and the plumber should be finished with the baths by the end of the day. Still waiting for the HVAC people to show up, though."

"What else is new?" I sigh. The AC hasn't been working for the last few weeks, and I've been trying to get the HVAC crew to take a look at it, but they always cancel on me at the last minute. I'm hoping they actually show up today or else I might have to look into working with a different company. Even with our industrial fans humming away in several of the bigger rooms and most of the windows open to encourage ventilation, the heat of the Louisiana summer is still brutal. My boys deserve better working conditions, and the new homeowners, however uppity, should get what they've paid for.

"I'll be glad when this place is done, and I don't have to smell that damn swamp all the time," Jose remarks. "I swear I can shower for an hour and still walk out stinking like this place."

I nod. I've noticed the same thing, like the stench of it clings wherever I go. "Soon," I assure him. "What else needs to be done?"

The foreman considers my question for a moment before listing off several projects that still need to get completed. Most of it's finishing work, and I'm glad to hear that we really are almost ready to wrap this thing up. At the end of the survey, Jose adds, "Oh, we've still got to fix that spot of drywall in the kitchen. You know, the one that got all torn up?"

I did know, better than anybody. Truthfully, I've been procrastinating on fixing that one. Even though I keep insisting that I'll do it myself, every time I go to start the project I get this cold feeling in my chest as though my heart is turning to ice. I keep revisiting the memory of that stormy night, that song, and that figure out in the swamp.

Speaking of storms, a low rumble of thunder rolls before either of us can say anything more. Almost immediately after, a burst of rain unleashes from the heavens, slamming against the brand new shingles of the roof like the drumming of a thousand fingers.

"Shit, the windows!" I exclaim, realizing that most of them are currently open. The last thing we need is for the rain to get in and waterlog the gorgeous new flooring and wallpaper.

Jose springs into action at the same time I do. "You take the upper floors," I call to him as he dashes further into the house. Within seconds, I hear him bellowing for everybody to start closing the windows. I do the same on the lower level, and a small army of workers disperses to complete the task at my direction.

But when the next peal of thunder hits, all hell breaks loose.

There's a loud thump outside, followed quickly by frenzied yelling from the upper floors. I sprint toward the stairs in time to catch Jose tearing down them, his face ashen and his eyes wide.

"What's going on?" I bark.

At the same time, he shouts, "Henri fell! He fucking fell!"

Before the words have time to sink in, Jose grabs me by the arm and hauls me toward the front door. Most of the crew isn't far behind as we burst out into the rain.

There's a lump on the ground a few feet away. For a moment, I don't understand what I'm looking at. But then the shape groans, and I realize with blossoming horror that I'm staring at a person.

My mind is still reeling to catch up to the terrible reality of the situation, but luckily my training kicks in, and my system shifts into autopilot. All of Hahnville's firefighters, including me, are licensed EMTs. I'm used to being the first on the scene and providing aid until an ambulance can respond.

Barely aware of the rain soaking through my clothes, I run over to the man on the ground. He's moaning in pain, but his body isn't moving. Jose follows me. He's talking quickly into his phone, already on the line with the 911 operator.

"Is he alive?" the foreman asks quickly, distress clinging to his features as he braces for the worst.

I nod, crouching down next to the man. It's Henri, all right, one of the kids who came to work for me right out of high school. His eyes are open and filled with terror as I try to assess the damage.

"Henri, can you hear me?" I ask.

"Yeah," he croaks, his voice strained as though it's costing him all his strength just to speak. "Am I gonna die?" he whispers.

"Not today," I tell him firmly, though I'm not sure yet if that's the truth. "You took a hell of a fall though." My eyes slide over him. I don't see anything obviously broken, and there's no blood. I glance up and note that the third story window is still open. He must have fallen from there.

"Ambulance is fifteen minutes out," Jose murmurs.

Fifteen minutes may not sound that long, but if somebody is bleeding internally, it can determine whether a patient lives or dies. I don't have any supplies with me, and I have no way of checking, so I can only hope that his injuries aren't that severe.

"Can you wiggle your fingers for me?" I ask. Relief surges through me as the kid obeys. "Now your toes," I tell him.

But Henri's booted feet don't move.

"I...I can't...." Henri breathes, staring up at me with horror dripping from his eyes.

"Hey, it's okay," I tell him, hoping that my voice doesn't portray my own panic. "Don't try to move. Lie as still as you can. The ambulance will be here soon."

There's not much more I can do for him after that except for stay crouched by his side, assuring him that he's going to be okay. The rain continues to hammer down as streaks of lightning jitter across the sky and thunder blossoms from the heavens.

At long last, I hear sirens in the distance.

I stay with Henri as a host of fire trucks, ambulances, and police cars congregate in the driveway. Emergency personnel swarm the area, and I do my best to keep my composure as I quietly tell the EMTs that I think the kid's back might be broken. The rest of my crew watches somberly as Henri is transferred onto a backboard and then a stretcher before finally disappearing into the back of an ambulance.

As soon as the ambulance tears down the driveway, sirens wailing, I turn to address my crew. Everybody is clearly spooked.

"I don't even know what to say," I begin in a shaky voice. "This is just... horrible. Jose, I want you to follow the ambulance to the hospital. I'll be there as soon as I can. I'm going to try to get ahold of Henri's dad. Everybody else, go home."

Moving like zombies, my crew follows my directions. I'm scrolling through my phone to find Henri's emergency contact information when I realize that one of the guys is lingering nearby, his eyes fixed to the open window above us.

"Boss?" the man asks tentatively, his gaze shifting down to meet mine.

"Yeah, Mike," I reply. I know he's buddies with Henri. This must be hitting him pretty hard.

"I was there when it happened," Mike says softly, his voice nearly drowned out by the pounding of the rain.

"It must have been terrible, seeing him fall like that," I sigh.

"Fall?" Mike shakes his head. "He didn't fall."

Fear sours in the pit of my stomach as Mike once again turns his wild gaze onto the window.

"He didn't fall," he repeats. "He was pushed."

15

___________

# MAKE IT GO AWAY

Bailey

"HOLY SHIT!" I whisper.

I'm sitting at one of the computers in the Hahnville Public Library, which doubles as the town's historical records center. After arguing with Tanner this morning, I'm now determined to find something, *anything*, to explain the things we've been experiencing. With the article that's currently on the screen in front of me, I think I may have just hit the jackpot.

Twenty-seven murders have been connected to the property in the better part of the last century.

I'm no expert in homicide statistics, but I'd bet good money that that number is way higher than the average.

As I skim the cramped text of the article, which is published on a sleek-looking true crime website, a pattern starts to emerge. Most of the victims were men from out of town. The vast majority of suspects were women, and all but six of the alleged murderers ended up in psychiatric facilities. The others had committed suicide before the police could catch up with them. All of the people involved had some sort of connection to the Gregory property.

My eyes widen as I pick out a familiar name in the mix of victims: Ashford. I picture the face of Penny's doctor, the one who had conspired with Vera to keep the old woman sedated and who had later been brutally murdered by his own wife.

Was it possible that Dr. Ashford's death had been related to the house?

I knew he hadn't been attacked near the swamp and that he had ultimately passed away in the hospital. Did that mean whatever was on the Gregory property wasn't bound to the land? I don't even want to think of the implications that would hold for Tanner and me.

Swallowing thickly, I force myself to keep reading.

After listing out the names of the dead, the author shifts from fact to speculation, noting some of the theories that have arisen over the years. This feels like safer territory. A lot of these conjectures are rumors I've heard over the years: the land is haunted, or cursed, or there are witches and demons in the swamp. But there's no proof for any of these, and I end up with more questions than answers by the time I'm finished reading.

I lean back in my chair and sigh.

I don't know what to make of all this. I've lived in Hahnville all my life, and of course I've heard the rumors that have swirled around the old Gregory place like dirty water down a drain. As kids, we'd whispered that the house was haunted and that a witch lived there. Even as Penny's day nurse, I'd hated being alone in the house after dark.

Could the land really be cursed or haunted?

I don't want to believe it, but I also can't think of a better explanation for all of the terrible things that have happened there over the years. My mind drifts back to Layla, who had refused to set foot on the property again after the fire that had consumed the main house and a good portion of the outbuildings.

Maybe I really should call her. As much as I hate to drag Layla back into the grips of whatever is happening here, a growing part of me understands that she's the only one who might have some of the answers I'm so desperately searching for.

*I'll call her tomorrow*, I decide.

The rest of my research doesn't bring up much new information. By mid-afternoon, I come to the conclusion that if there is anything more to uncover, I won't find it here. I take a moment to print out the article, thank the librarian, and then step out into the overcast heat. The sky is dark and crowded with purplish clouds, heralding an impending storm.

Luck is on my side, and I manage to make it home just as the skies open up. Thunder crashes with an intensity that I can feel in my bones. The atmosphere is electric, as though the very air that I breathe is somehow alive. Although I don't know why, I realize that I'm frightened, my body anticipating that something terrible is about to happen.

I don't want to give in to that feeling, so I drop my research on the kitchen table before retreating to the bedroom with my laptop to watch some mindless reality TV until it's time to go to work.

I'm on my third episode of some silly dating show when I hear the front door creak open over the roar of the storm.

"Tanner?" I call, my heartbeat galloping as I strain to pick up any unusual sounds. "Is that you?"

To my immense relief, he calls back, "Yeah."

Confusion floods through me then. It's only 4:00 in the afternoon, and Tanner doesn't usually get home until right before I leave for my shift at 7:00. What is he doing here so early?

When Tanner appears in the doorway of the bedroom, I'm sure that something terrible has occurred. His face is etched with fear, and he looks older somehow, as though he's aged several years since our fight this morning. A haunted gleam lingers in his eyes as he fixes his gaze on me.

"What happened?" I ask, my voice little more than a whisper.

Tanner runs his hands over his face and shakes his head. After a long moment, he finally replies, "There was an accident at the job site."

"An accident?" I gasp. "Is everybody all right?"

"I don't know," he sighs. I wait for him to tell me more, but he doesn't elaborate. Instead, he kicks off his boots and starts unbuttoning his shirt, which is damp and wrinkled as though he's been standing in the rain.

I'm not sure why, but my gut tells me to tread carefully. I wait until he shucks the shirt into the laundry hamper and perches on the edge of the mattress before I probe, "Are you okay?"

His eyes snap to mine, and it's like there's a war going on inside of him. After a moment too long, he answers, "I don't know." His tone is flat, and the weight of it makes my skin crawl. Whatever he's seen today, it wasn't good. Maybe he's in shock, I consider.

Tentatively, I reach out to take his hand. He flinches as my fingers brush his wrist, but before I can draw back, he clutches my palm and brings my hand to his bare chest. The desperate thud of his heartbeat radiates through my fingers, and my mind conjures up an image of a deer, frozen and panting, in the headlights of on an oncoming car.

"What happened?" I ask again, shifting to rest beside him on the edge of the bed. "Please, Tanner, just tell me."

He closes his eyes and draws in a hitched breath. "It could have been me," he whispers, naked terror saturating his voice. "It could have been *you*."

Before I can ask him what he means, he closes the distance between us and claims my mouth in a searing kiss. I stiffen at first, confused and a little frightened, but then I remind myself that this is Tanner, the man I love. He's not making any sense, and I still don't understand what's happened, but I can feel the desperation as his lips pull at mine.

I kiss him back, throwing caution to the wind. He needs this, I know it in my bones. Hell, maybe I need this too, especially after our fight this morning.

As soon as he feels me respond, Tanner uses his weight to flip me back onto the bed so that my back is pressed into the mattress as his toned form looms over me. He stares down at me, his eyes bright and wild like he's in the grips of a fever.

"You're mine," he breathes in a voice so low it's barely audible over the storm. He punctuates his words with a thrust of his hips, and I can't help but moan as his concealed hardness brushes against my core. "Say it," he growls, rolling his hips again. "Say it."

"I'm yours!" I moan, arching my back off the bed in an attempt to find a better angle.

He leans down, the planes of his muscled chest hard against my clothed breasts. His teeth nip at my ear, and I sigh. "You're mine," he repeats, his hot breath fanning the tender skin of my neck. "You're mine."

He wastes no time undressing me as I writhe beneath him. He gathers the hem of my blouse and tugs it unceremoniously over my head. Next, his quick fingers unclasp my bra, releasing my breasts. He takes one peaked nipple in his mouth as his hands work at the zipper of my shorts before sliding the denim down my toned legs.

Soon, I'm entirely naked, every inch of skin exposed to him. He drinks in the sight of me with bright, hungry eyes. Without dragging his gaze from mine, he steps out of his jeans and boxers, freeing his cock.

Anticipation builds as he slides the head of it through my slick folds. I sigh with pleasure as he moves against me, but it's not enough. I want more.

I buck my hips against him, urging him forward. Obeying my wordless command, he positions himself at my entrance and, just when I'm about to whine in frustration, he slams into me hard.

"Fuck!" I gasp at the sudden fullness. I half expect Tanner to pause to give me a moment to adjust to his size, but instead, he draws back and immediately thrusts back in.

The painful pleasure of it is like nothing I've ever felt before. I moan as he pistons into me, hitting just the right angle with every stroke, and he stifles the sound with his mouth against mine.

I can feel myself rising closer to the precipice with every thrust, and soon I whisper, "I'm so close, Tanner."

His quickens the rhythm, coaxing me closer and closer until I tumble over the edge with an ecstatic cry. Tanner doesn't stop though. Instead, he presses his forehead against mine as I feel him begin to twitch inside me.

"You're mine," slips from his mouth as his hips stutter from his own release.

We lie there listening to the storm in silence until my phone alarm alerts me that I have to leave for work.

By the time I'm dressed and presentable, Tanner is asleep. I kiss his brow softly, not wanting to wake him, before crossing over to the door.

But something makes me linger on the threshold. It's as though something in the air behind me has shifted, and my neck prickles with the sensation that somebody is watching me.

I turn slowly, squinting against the stormy dimness. There's nobody else in the room except for Tanner, who's still asleep in bed.

A flash of lightning pierces the gloom, and for a moment, Tanner's face isn't his own. The thing that isn't Dalton stares back at me, the corners of its mouth upturned in a rictus grin.

Panicked, I slap the light switch, immediately bathing the room in a warm glow.

The face is gone, leaving only Tanner sleeping soundly in bed.

I turn again to leave, and this time, I don't look back.

# 16

# SOMETHING'S OUT THERE

Tanner

THREE STORIES IS a hell of a long way down.

I'm standing at the window Henri fell from, my feet planted where his must have been less than twenty-four hours before. I imagine the pressure of two hands on my shoulder blades, of the sudden weightlessness as gravity takes hold. Had Henri been afraid while he was falling? Or had been too surprised to even realize what was happening? What would it feel like to fly for just a moment?

*Why don't you try it and see?*

The thought scratches at the edge of my brain, and before I can even process it, one of my hands reaches out toward the closed frame of the window.

"Tyler?" a voice calls from the room behind me.

I jolt, the sudden sound tugging me back from the window. My mind races as I realize what I had been doing, and I try to keep the fear off my face as I turn to the speaker.

Jake Carter, the new owner of the Gregory place, is standing in the doorway with his arms crossed. Anger radiates off him in sour waves, and I can't help but judge him for being pissed that the construction is behind schedule rather than worried for the guy who was injured. Behind him, his wife lingers in the hallway.

"Tyler, what the hell is going on here?" Jake asks. I'm the only one here, so it's clear that he's talking to me even though he got my name wrong.

I have to stifle the urge to roll my eyes. "Tanner," I correct. "And what's going on is exactly what I told you over the phone."

I had, of course, called Jake late last night as soon as Henri's dad had updated me on the kid's condition. Jake had sounded drunk, and I have a sneaking suspicion that he's asking again now because he had too much alcohol in his system to remember yesterday's discussion.

"Will he be okay? The guy who fell, I mean," Jake's wife asks from her spot in the corridor. Her eyes are trained on the window, and she looks as though she's afraid that some unseen force will suck her out of it if she gets too close.

"He'll live," I tell her. "They got him into emergency surgery yesterday evening, and his dad said he's pulling through okay. His back's broken, but they're not sure how bad it is yet."

"That's horrible," the wife gasps. I struggle to remember her name. Is it Julie? No, Julia, I recall. She follows up by asking, "Is there anything we can do for him?"

My eyes flick over her figure as she lingers just outside the threshold. I'd wager that her tailored dress and sleek pumps probably cost more than some of my construction equipment, and her perfect hair and nails definitely aren't the kind to come cheap. She looks like she should be sipping martinis in Hampton Beach, not standing in an unfinished house on the edge of a derelict swamp in Louisiana. Given her appearance, I'm frankly shocked that she genuinely seems upset about Henri's condition.

But Jake's reaction is exactly as expected. "We shouldn't have to pay anything," he snaps. "He was one of your people, and with what

I'm paying you, safety should already be part of the package. Anybody who gets injured from your team is your responsibility."

I do roll my eyes at that. "This ain't about liability," I spit back. Of course with these yuppie types, it's all about the money. Jake clearly couldn't care less that Henri might never walk again. "Like I said last night, it was an accident."

*Was it?*

There's that little voice again, sliding around the corners of my thoughts. My mind drifts back to yesterday's conversation with Mike. He had been so sure that Henri had been pushed, that somebody else had been in the room with them. Despite the heat of the day, goosebumps prickle up my arms at the memory of Mike's haunted expression.

"Whatever," Jake waves away sourly. "Just so long as some redneck doesn't try to sue me later."

I open my mouth to snarl something rude at the man, but before I can speak, Julia admonishes, "Don't be nasty, Jake."

"I'm just being pragmatic," he insists, doubling down. "Anyway, since we're here, you might as well walk us through. It looks like we're almost done, right?"

Using the collective term, as though Jake had been right here beside my crew the entire time, has me bristling, but I remind myself that this is the guy cutting our checks, so I need to play nice. Reining in my hostility, I reply, "Yep, only a few more weeks, and then we'll be finished. Let me take you around."

As we work our way down, Jake grows calmer as he confirms that everything is to his liking on the third and second floors. Julia, on the other hand, settles into the stereotype I had first applied to her.

"Are you sure that this is real marble?" she quizzes, running one manicured hand over the countertop in one of the second floor bathrooms. "It feels a little plasticky, don't you think?"

I shake my head, internally fuming. "I can assure you that it's exactly what you ordered, ma'am."

She nods, momentarily satisfied until her eyes land on the floor, and she asks, "Is it just me, or is the gap between the tiling a little wide?"

The commentary gets worse once we make it down to the ground floor. While Jake remains largely uncaring, Julia frets over every little detail. The most painful part is when we get to the kitchen.

I immediately want to kick myself as her gaze falls on the section of broken drywall. I was going to fix it yesterday, but then Henri's fall had completely distracted me. Truthfully, I hadn't even thought about it again until now.

"What happened here?" Jake asks, his eyes narrowing.

"An animal got in a while ago, I think. It was on the schedule to be fixed yesterday, but I sent my crew home after the accident," I explain. "I'm going to take care of it once y'all leave."

Jake doesn't seem convinced. "I'm not paying you to send your people home when there's shit like this that needs doing," he jabs.

"It'll get done," I insist, once again tamping down my anger.

Luckily, Julia changes the subject before Jake can press the issue. "It's awfully hot in here," she remarks, pulling at the collar of her dress.

This feels like safer territory. "The HVAC people are coming out soon. Don't worry, it'll be like the Arctic in here by the time you move in," I tell her in a placating tone.

"And what about the outbuildings?" Jake asks. "How's the garage coming?"

"Follow me, and I'll show you," I reply. The garage is an easy win for me, since it's completely finished and just waiting for Jake's multiple flashy sports cars to be parked in it. We trudge outside into the glaring morning sunlight. Even though it's not even noon yet, the air of the swamp shimmers with a greenish haze.

"This place gives me the creeps," Julia remarks as she picks her way carefully across the driveway toward the garage. She nods out to the cluster of sinking gravestones that jut up from the muck like the teeth of some gaping maw. "Do you think it's haunted?"

My breath sticks in my chest at her words. Before I can say anything, Jake laughs. "Don't be stupid. Of course it isn't haunted."

"Some people think it is," I counter. "There have always been stories about this place, about the swamp."

The woman pauses as an uneasy shadow flickers across her delicate features. "What kind of stories?" she presses.

Jake once again cuts me off. "Who gives a shit?" he chuckles. "Ghosts, witches, werewolves—that's all kid stuff. The only thing we should be afraid of is the IRS."

Julia glances over at me. I can tell she wants to know more, but she doesn't want to ask in front of her husband. I can't blame her.

I follow Jake over to the garage. He and I discuss the finer points of the structure while Julia lingers in the driveway poking at her phone. I nod along as Jake boasts about his collection of very expensive and fast cars, pretending to pay attention as my mind drifts to stories surrounding the swamp.

Bailey had shared her research with me this morning before I came here. I was shocked to see how many people had died on or around the old Gregory place. In my opinion, Henri was probably lucky not to have been one of them.

It makes sense that there's something unnatural haunting the property, especially after yesterday.

When I had come home to Bailey, I had gotten the distinct impression that something had been watching her. As I had lost myself in her body, I had repeated my claim over her, that she was mine, and I was hers. Whatever had been there with us had needed to hear it. *I* had needed to hear it.

Whatever the thing is, it seems to go for the women and drive them to kill the men in their lives. That much is obvious from Bailey's research. I'm worried that it will get to her, but last night showed me that she's still herself, at least for now.

"Jake! Jake, come quick!"

Julia's shrill scream has us both tearing out of the garage and away from my troubled thoughts.

"What? What happened?" Jake yells as he and I skid to his wife's side.

"There's somebody in the swamp!" she cries, pointing out in the direction of the cemetery.

We turn to follow the direction of her finger, but there's nothing there, not even a shadow.

"Don't be crazy," Jake huffs, immediately brushing away his wife's concern. "You probably saw a bird or something."

But I have a terrible feeling that whatever she saw, it wasn't an animal.

"It's probably just one of the neighbors out for a walk or some kids trying to get a look at the house," I tell her, though I don't really believe that. But what else am I supposed to say? That it's a ghost? Worried she might want to look herself, I add, "I'll go check though."

Echoes of the night of the thunderstorm snap at my thoughts as I trudge across the brittle lawn to the mouth of the swamp. My fingers itch at the memory of the figure that had dissolved into the mire beneath my touch. Surely, I'm safe in the daylight under the watchful eyes of my clients, right?

Steeling myself, I step into the marsh. The earth is treacherous beneath my feet, but I choose my steps carefully and manage to avoid most of the deeper areas. A few minutes later, I use the gnarled arm of a cypress tree to haul myself onto the small outcropping of the cemetery.

It's empty.

"Nobody here!" I call, squinting over my shoulder at Jake and Julia, who haven't moved an inch. I can't read their expressions from here, but Jake shoots me a thumbs up.

I turn to leave, but a flicker among the trunks of the cypress trees catches my eyes.

There's a shadow there, about my size. I can barely make out its features through the haze, but I can tell it's wearing a funny sort of a coat, like something you'd see in a historical reenactment.

And then for a brief moment, the clouds shift and the light catches the figure's face.

*Dalton.*

Well, kind of.

It looks like a bad wax figure of him, stuck in the uncanny valley between natural and unnatural. Whatever it is, it's definitely not human.

And when it raises its misshapen hand to wave, the only thing I can do is scream.

# 17

# VISIONS OF EVIL

Bailey

THIS CAN'T BE REAL.

My heart thuds against my ribs as my eyes dart around the familiar space. Everything is the same as it was before the fire. The wallpaper, lovingly restored by Dalton, is fresh and vibrant. The surface of the dining room table gleams as though it's just been polished. Warm yellow light spills down from the chandelier, the crystal beads clinking delicately amidst a backdrop of suffocating silence.

It's Miss Penny's dining room at the old Gregory place.

Logically, I know I can't really be here. *Here* doesn't even exist anymore. I watched the flames consume the house, tearing at the old wooden frame with a thousand grasping fingers. The heat was unbearable, and I coughed for weeks afterward from breathing in so much smoke.

So how am I here?

The last thing I remember is going to sleep after coming home from my night shift. So this must be a dream. There's nothing else it can be. And yet...

I stare at the table, which should be burned to a crisp along with the rest of the house. A chair is pulled out, waiting for me.

I take a step toward it. I'm screaming at myself to stop, but my legs seem to move of their own accord, dragging me closer and closer until I fall roughly into the seat. The wooden edges dig into my thighs and back, sharp and cool against my skin.

There's a creaking noise behind me. It's the unmistakable sound of footsteps crossing the tired floorboards from the kitchen to the dining room. Horror trickles down my spine, alighting my nerves and urging my heartbeat to a gallop. I try desperately to turn my head to see who's approaching me, but I can't. My muscles are stuck tight. It's like my body is betraying me.

It's all I can do to squeak out, "Who's there?"

Goosebumps break out across my arms and legs as a low, masculine chuckle thrums through the room. The footsteps stop directly behind me, the stranger standing so close to me that I can feel his breath, hot and oppressive, fanning against my skin.

"Hello, Bailey," a voice croons in my ear.

"Who are you?" I whisper, still unable to move.

"Maybe I'm Tanner," the stranger suggests. Feather-light fingers ghost over the exposed skin of my neck, and I gasp in surprise. "Maybe I'm Dalton." The digits brush my collarbone. "Or maybe I'm something else entirely."

Before I have time to react, the hand closes around one of my shoulders and shoves me forward, propelling me out of the chair and up against the hard edge of the dining room table. I yelp at the sudden movement as the stranger bends me over the wooden surface, pinning me down with a firm hand on my back.

I squirm against his hold, but he's way too strong.

Another chuckle erupts behind me, and I freeze as the stranger nudges my legs apart and steps in between them. Only then do I realize how exposed I am. I'm only wearing a thin satin nightgown and a pair of lace panties, and now, bent over the table, I can feel the stranger's body pressing against my core.

"Are you scared, Bailey?" he asks, his velvet voice laced with poison.

"No," I say, even though I know he can feel me trembling against him.

"Good girls don't tell lies," the stranger hisses in my ear. "But we both know you're not a good girl, are you?"

Anger swells in me, overtaking the fear. "Who are you?" I spit. "What do you want?"

"So impatient," he murmurs. He nuzzles his face into my hair, and I cringe against his hold. "Are you that eager to be mine?"

"I'm not yours," I snarl. "I'll never be yours!"

I don't even think about what I do next. It's purely instinctual, fueled by some distant part of my brain coaxed alive by the fear that's pulsing through my veins.

I shove both of my elbows behind me, catching the stranger in the ribs. He staggers backward just enough for me to turn in his grasp.

Everything stills as I catch sight of his face.

The thing that's not Dalton stares back, it's lips upturned in a mockery of a smile. Crooked, sharp teeth line its mouth. Its eyes are dark, the type of black that seems to gobble up the light, and they're locked on me.

"What the fuck are you?" I breathe, terror permeating the curve of my words.

Its grin widens.

"It's time to wake up, Bailey," the thing says. Its mouth doesn't move in time with its voice, like its movements are lagging a split second behind the sound it produces.

It raises one hand and snaps its fingers.

The transition between sleep and wakefulness is sudden and shocking.

One moment, I'm in the dining room of the old Gregory place, withering under the gaze of the thing that's not Dalton.

The next, I'm sitting up in bed, panting and shaking and ready to puke my guts out.

It's a race against the bile rising in my throat as I desperately kick myself free of the tangled sheets and dash into the bathroom. I make it to the toilet just in time to empty the contents of my stomach into the bowl.

Once I'm done retching, I sink down onto the bathroom floor, relishing the cool smoothness of the tile against my overheated skin. Sweat beads on my forehead and the small of my back. My muscles tremble as they had in the dream, and my heart flutters like a hummingbird's from the adrenaline running through my system.

"It was a nightmare," I whisper to myself. For the sake of my sanity, I'm not even going to try to consider any other possibilities.

Standing on shaky legs, I stagger over to the sink and turn on the cold water. I run my hands under the stream for a moment before splashing the cool liquid against my face. As it drips back down into the basin, I imagine that it's the nightmare sloughing off me, swirling away down the drain and far, far away.

I take a few deep breaths to steady myself before straightening up and grabbing my toothbrush. But when my eyes flash to the mirror, I catch a glimpse of a face – *its face* – reflected there, floating just over my shoulder.

Letting out an ungodly screech, I whip around and reflexively fling my toothbrush at the thing.

There's nothing there.

The toothbrush sails through empty air and clatters on the floor.

"Fuck you!" I scream, kicking the spot where the thing had been.

I feel like I'm going crazy. My mind races as I claw my way out to the bedroom. I try to slow my breathing and quiet my racing thoughts, but it's a Herculean task. After several minutes of counting my inhales and exhales, I calm down and locate my phone, which is still plugged into the outlet beside the bed.

My first instinct is to call Tanner. But instead, I find myself dialing a different number.

The line rings two times before somebody picks up. "Hey Bailey, what's up?" a cheerful, familiar voice greets me.

"Layla," I sigh, relief crashing over me at the sound of her familiar accent.

"That's me," my friend agrees, sounding thoroughly confused and a little bit concerned. "Bailey, are you okay?"

"Yeah," I say. I try to muster up some more enthusiasm, pushing the panic away. "Yeah, everything's fine. I was just calling to see how you're doing."

"I'm great," Layla replies, though I can tell she's not totally convinced by my answer.

I struggle to find a topic that has nothing to do with the nightmare I've just lived through. Finally I ask, "You're liking Florida?"

"Uh-huh! It's awesome. There's so much to do!" Layla gushes. "I've got a great nursing job, and we're renting such a cute little house. I can't wait until you can get some time off to visit!"

"I'd love to come down," I reply earnestly. The thought of leaving Hahnville, of fleeing this thing, is so tantalizing. I think back to our failed trip to NOLA. Maybe we hadn't gone far enough. Would it leave us alone if we put enough distance between us and the swamp? Something tells me it will never stop, but part of me wants to grab Tanner and run. I decide that I'll talk to him this weekend, see if I can convince him to get the hell out of here.

"How's everything in town?" Layla inquires, breaking me from my reverie. "Is everybody behaving?"

"No more than usual," I joke. "I did take a new job though."

"Ooh, spill!"

"You remember the Wilsons?"

"Of course," Layla confirms. They were really kind to her after the house burned down. They had assisted in finding a suitable living situation for Miss Penny, and they had basically taken Layla and Dalton in until they could shift their lives to Florida.

"Well, Robert had a pretty gnarly fall a little while ago. His leg's pretty messed up. Helen's got me coming over for night shifts so she can get some sleep," I relay.

Layla gasps. "Oh my god! How'd it happen?"

"He said he was out for a walk and fell in the marsh." It's not exactly a lie, but it's not the full truth either.

Luckily for me, my friend doesn't pry any further. "I'll call Helen and check on him," she promises. "How's his prognosis?"

"His recovery will be pretty long and painful, but I think he'll be able to walk again," I tell her. I take a deep breath and then ask her the question I've been holding in since I first called. "How's Dalton?"

"Oh, ya know, still sexy as hell," she giggles. "He's started doing freelance work around the city so he's earning his keep. You should see the houses he's restored. Some of these places are like gold toilet level of ridiculous!"

"So he's mostly in Florida these days?"

"Yep," she confirms. "Actually, hang on. He's right here, I'll put you on speaker!

A second later, Dalton–the real Dalton–speaks. "Hey Bailey!" he says.

"Hi," I respond weakly, dread pooling in the pit of my stomach. There's no excuse now. Whatever I've been seeing, it definitely isn't Dalton. Part of me has known that all along, but now there's no more wiggle room, no room for doubt.

I can't really pay attention to the rest of the call. The words we exchange pass in a blur until I look at the clock on the bedside and realize I have to start getting ready for work.

"I have to go," I say. "Talk soon?"

"Of course," Layla assures me. "Bye!"

"Bye!" I echo before ending the call.

I sit on the edge of the bed for a moment, just listening to the silence. After a few seconds, I sigh. I really do have to start moving if I want to make it to Helen's in time for my shift.

Standing demands massive effort, and I trudge towards the bathroom wondering how the hell I'm supposed to get through an entire night of work after all the things that have happened today.

I've made it a few steps away when my phone rings. Layla's name flashes across the screen. Figuring that she must've forgotten to tell me something, I answer the call without hesitation.

For a moment, nothing comes through the speakers but a weird crackling noise.

And then the music starts, flooding down the line and blasting out into the room at a decibel I didn't know my phone was capable of.

*Folks, I'm goin' down to St. James Infirmary, see my baby there...*

I press the button to end the call, but nothing happens.

*She's stretched out on a long, white table, so sweet, so cold, so fair...*

18

---

# CHAT WITH THE DEVIL

Tanner

"YOU WANT A HAND WITH THAT, BOSS?"

I glance up from the section of wall I'm measuring in the kitchen and smile thinly at Jose. "Nah, I've got it," I tell him. "Thanks though."

"If you're sure." The foreman shrugs. His eyes flicker to the window and the setting sun beyond. "Do you at least want some company? Being alone in this place in the dark would give me the creeps."

"I'll be fine," I assure Jose with confidence that I don't quite feel. In truth, I would rather not be here at all, let alone after nightfall, but the contract is on the line. I can't afford for Jake to come up for a surprise visit and find the kitchen wall still scratched up. He'd probably fire me on the spot.

The foreman doesn't seem quite convinced, but still he turns to leave. "Just call me if shit gets weird," he throws over his shoulder. "See ya on Monday!"

"Later," I toss back.

I lean against the wall and listen as Jose bustles out of the house, crunches across the gravel driveway, and gets in his truck. Soon enough, the door slams, the engine starts, and he rolls down the driveway into the descending gloom of the evening.

Anxiety prickles over my skin as the growl of his vehicle fades into the distance. I'm acutely aware that I'm alone here in this building, festering on the edge of the swamp.

But am I really the only one out here?

Yesterday's excursion into the marsh surfaces unbidden to the forefront of my thoughts. I can recall the horrible figure perfectly, down to its treacherous smile and the way its nimble hand waved, beckoning me deeper in the mire.

I shrieked like a little girl and booked it back to my clients as quickly as I could. Julia's eyes were wide with fear, but Jake scoffed at me for getting startled by an animal in the swamp.

An animal. A gator, actually. That's what I told them I'd seen. It sounded better than telling them I encountered a ghost or demon out among the sinking tombstones.

Jake laughed his ass off, and I feigned embarrassment at my unmanly behavior, but I could tell that his wife suspected I was lying, though she simply pursed her lips and remained silent. Soon after, they left without further incident, and I hightailed it out of there as soon as I could.

Now I'm back, and this time there's nobody to run to.

Thoroughly unnerved, I decide I won't just sit here in silence. I drag the heavy radio over from the sitting room and set it up on the kitchen counter, turning it to a local country station. I crank up the volume loud enough to drown out the burgeoning chatter of insects and the groan of the cypress trees swaying in the evening breeze, the soundtrack of the swamp.

Not wanting to have to stay any longer than necessary, I pick up my stud finder and get to work. First, I mark the areas where I need to stay away from with a pencil. The next thing I do is grab the pry bar and leverage the molding away from the bottom of the wall, revealing the seam between the floor and the sheetrock.

Now I'm ready for the fun part. Drywall removal is dusty work. I've already prepped the room by laying drop cloths on the floor and counters. All I have to do is find my respirator and I'll be able to start knocking down this wall so I can respace the studs.

I swear I had left it on the counter when I had come in this morning, but the covered surface is completely barren. One of the other guys must have thought it was theirs, I figure. It's not a big deal. I'll check in with the crew on Monday to make sure I get it back, but in the meantime, I know I have an extra in my truck.

The thought of going outside to retrieve it makes me pause.

My mind skitters back to the figure in the swamp. There's no way I'm going out there, alone and defenseless, with that thing running around in the dark.

I consider the situation for a second before grabbing a hammer from my toolkit. It's not exactly a gun, but it'll do.

Hefting the makeshift weapon in my hand, I weave my way out of the house. I hesitate for a moment at the threshold, my eyes scanning the empty driveway. Nothing looks amiss. The night is alive with the normal sounds of the swamp now that I can hear them clearly over the distant blare of the radio.

"Hello?" I call into the darkness.

To my immense relief, there's no response.

I draw in a deep breath, steeling myself, and then step out into the night.

Gravel crunches beneath my feet. The sound is deafening against the relative stillness of the swamp. I cringe with each step as I pick my way over to my truck, which is thankfully only a few feet away down the driveway.

As I approach the vehicle, I weigh my options. What if I just got in the truck and went home? I could come back on Monday and finish the kitchen amidst the bustle of my crew.

*Coward.*

The thought slithers across my brain and down my spine.

I don't want to prove it right.

Pushing any ideas of retreating away, I fumble with my keys, ultimately managing to unlock the truck's back door with shaking hands. I'm pretty sure the respirator is somewhere in the cramped bench seat. Bailey's always telling me to get my stuff organized back there, and I'm kicking myself now that I haven't listened to her suggestion sooner. I feel more and more on edge as I paw through my equipment until finally my hand closes around the mask of the respirator.

"Thank god," I sigh in relief.

I straighten up, pulling the respirator with me, and slam the door of the truck closed. After locking it, I turn to head back into the house.

And then I freeze.

Somebody is standing in the doorway, silhouetted by the light spilling out from the hallway.

Fear and rage cascade through me, shoving away any hope for rational thought. A frenzied roar escapes my throat as I throw the respirator down and brandish the hammer, barreling forward toward the intruder.

The figure doesn't budge.

When I'm only a few inches from it, I swing the hammer with all the force I can muster.

The head of the weapon catches the light as it arcs through the air and comes down to hit...

Nothing.

There's absolutely nothing there.

Momentum propels me forward, and I stagger into the hallway, reeling until I can catch my balance again.

I stand there for a moment, listening for any sign of the intruder. I see nothing out of the ordinary, but the hairs on my arms and the back of my neck prickle as though there are eyes boring into me.

"Show yourself, you bastard!" I bellow. My voice ricochets

through the empty building, and that's when I realize that the radio is no longer playing.

Adrenaline surges through my veins as I storm toward the kitchen. I burst into the room, expecting another trick.

But the thing that leans idly against the damaged wall is no mirage.

It's the same figure from the swamp. It looks exactly as I remember, as though it had stepped straight from my thoughts and into the bright light of the kitchen.

I stand in the doorway, my eyes fixed on its unwavering gaze. It smiles to reveal a set of crooked, pointed teeth.

"Good evening," it says, tipping its head slightly. Its voice is like the rustle of leaves in the underbrush. Nothing normal sounds like that. Nothing *alive.*

"Who are you?" I demand. Fear betrays the acid in my voice as I tighten my grip around the hammer.

The thing's smile widens. "I've gone by many names over the years," it lilts in that horrible reedy voice. "But you can call me Amos."

"*What* are you?" I snarl.

Grinning, it replies, "I'm the swamp, and everything in it. I'm the thunder and the sunshine and everything in between. Always have been, always will be."

"What do you want with me?" I'm stuck between terror and disbelief. This can't be real, and yet my senses tell me that it is. I'm not dreaming. I'm very much awake.

"You?" Amos lets out something that might be a laugh. I fight the urge to slap my hands over my ears at the sound. "It's not you I want," it croons, taking a step toward me. Every muscle in my body is tense and straining, but I don't back down.

"Then what?"

Amos cocks its head, sizing me up. Finally it answers, "This land is mine. I've been here for a very long time. All who pass through or settle here have fed me over the years, nourishing me with their pain and desire. I was strong, so strong, and then…the flames!" Its voice rises to a shrill wail as it doubles over, clutching at itself with spidery fingers. "I'm so hungry! So hungry!"

Every inch of me trembles. My fight or flight instinct is gone. I am frozen in place, unable to escape from the nightmare unraveling in front of me.

In a sudden flurry of movement, the thing snaps upright again, its face once again placid. Its eyes, matte black and empty, wheedle into mine. "I'll give you anything you desire," Amos murmurs in a sugary tone. "Fame, money, power– it can all be yours. All I ask is one thing in return." Pale hands stretch out to me in a supplicating gesture, the fingertips so close they almost brush my chest.

When I find the will to speak, all I can muster is a horrified whisper. "What? What do you want?"

It grins again. "The girl."

Horror tears through me as I realize it's talking about Bailey. It's enough to shatter me from my stupor.

"Never!" I growl. I toss myself forward, once again swinging the hammer into the air. This time, I'll make sure not to miss.

Fingers, somehow both hot and freezing at the same time, close around my wrist, jerking my arm back. I yelp in pain as my shoulder joint wrenches in the socket. At the same time, the thing catches me around the throat with the other hand, squeezing cruelly as it raises me into the air as if I weigh nothing. My dangling feet scramble to find purchase on the ground, but my boots only swing uselessly in the air.

"It'll have to be the hard way then," Amos drawls, eyes locked on mine.

In spite of the fingers digging into my neck and the palm crushing my windpipe, I manage to croak out, "Go to hell!"

Amos leans forward until our noses are almost touching. Rancid breath fans across my face as the thing smiles.

"Don't worry," Amos hisses. "You're about to."

19

———————

# THAT'S NOT TANNER

Bailey

TANNER DIDN'T COME HOME last night.

It's evident as soon as I step through the front door after my night shift at the Wilson's. At barely past 6:00 in the morning, I should hear him snoring away or bustling in the kitchen getting breakfast ready, but my ears are met only with silence.

"Tanner?" I call, even though I know in my bones that there's nobody here to answer.

Unease creeps beneath my skin as I hang up my purse on the hook beside the door and kick off my shoes. There's still no movement in the depths of our home, and as I wander from room to room, I realize that nothing's changed since I left the night before. The bed's in disarray, the sheets tangled and the comforter crumpled halfway onto the floor. The dishes in the sink are untouched, food in the fridge uneaten. Emptiness hangs in the air, vacant and suffocating.

Where could he be?

I stop in the doorway to the bedroom. Even my phone is still on the bedside table, plugged into the outlet. After it kept playing that horrible song last night, I had simply abandoned it and run out the door, stopping only to grab my purse and the car keys on the way out.

Maybe Tanner had tried to call me? It's the only thing I can think of. There might be a text message or a voicemail waiting for me.

I start forward, but then a memory of that horrible face flashes through my thoughts, and a sudden bolt of fear stops me from entering. Could the thing that isn't Dalton still be here?

I stare into the empty space. Beams of early morning sun filter in through the curtains, chasing away the shadows. Nothing moves.

My eyes fall on my phone. It's face down on the bedside table, blissfully quiet.

Steeling myself, I take a step into the room and then another. My heart thrums frantically at the thought that my phone could erupt into that sinister music at any moment as I inch closer and closer.

Finally, I can't put it off any longer. I reach out and gingerly flip the device over, pressing the button to see if I've got any notifications.

Nothing.

No calls. No messages. No word from Tanner.

"Where the hell are you?" I mutter as I tug my phone free from the charger.

I sink down onto the bed and groan at the feeling of the soft mattress beneath my body. Between the nightmares and the long hours I've spent awake in the dark, the exhaustion is starting to take a toll on me. I ease myself back so that I'm propped on the pillows. Once I'm comfortable, I type out a quick text to Tanner.

*Where are you? Are you okay?*

With a quick tap of my finger, I send the message off into the void. Hopefully, Tanner will see it soon, wherever he is. As I scroll through my social media, I decide that I'll give him half an hour. If I don't hear from him by then, I'll try calling.

About halfway through the agonizing wait, I drift off. My dreams are fuzzy with the green haze of the swamp, and when I'm startled awake almost an hour later, I swear I can smell it.

The scent of the mire crawls through the air, and I hold my hand up to my nose as I realize that this is not just some remnant of an inarticulate nightmare. Blinking sleep from my eyes, I squint out at the room.

"Holy shit!" I gasp as my eyes fall on a figure looming in the bedroom door. My heart skips a beat before I realize who it is. "Tanner?"

He doesn't move.

I sit up, running my hands over my face. The fetid stench of the marsh starts to fade, but the dread that accompanies it does not. My pulse races as I study Tanner's form lingering in the doorway. He's dressed in the same clothes as yesterday, and he's muddy up to his knees as if he's been wading out in the swamp. His hair is disheveled. To my horror, I notice a ring of angry purple bruises marring the skin of his neck.

"Baby, what happened to you?" I gasp, wrestling my limbs free of the sheets. I want to go to him, comfort him, but a little voice in the back of my head whispers that something is wrong here.

But how could Tanner possibly be dangerous?

I shake the thought away as I force myself to stand on trembling legs and walk toward him.

He remains motionless as I grow near. His eyes, alight with a strange, feverish glint, track my movements. Beneath his shirt, his muscles are tense and straining. His whole body is like a coiled spring, ready to snap at any moment, and I can't hold back the thrill of fear that reverberates through my limbs.

When I'm an arm's length away, I stop.

He looks worse up close. If we hadn't spent so much time together, I'd think that he'd gone on a bender. But I know better than that. Something terrible has happened to him, and I'm willing to bet that it has everything to do with the old Gregory place.

"Who did this to you?" I whisper. I lift my hand to his collarbone, ghosting my fingertips over the mottled bruises there. "What did you see?"

"The truth," he utters. The words hang between us as I struggle to understand what he means. Finally, he breaks his preternatural stillness and wraps his arms around me, pulling me forward until I'm flush against his broad chest.

My body melts against his. Even the swampy smell that clings to his shirt doesn't deter me. I close my eyes and snake my arms around his middle, enjoying how solid he feels in my embrace.

Remembering the promise I made to myself the previous evening, I tell him, "I talked to Layla yesterday."

His muscles stiffen. "Layla," he parrots. It's not a question. He says the name wistfully, as if recalling an old friend. Once again, unease blooms in the pit of my stomach, though I can't quite pinpoint why.

"She asked if we want to come visit," I continue. "I...I think we should. I think we should go."

Tanner's arms contract around me, his grip tightening. "We can't," he pushes back in a flat tone. "I have to finish the house."

"No," I insist. "Let Jose take over. I just want to get out of here, Tanner. Something happened yesterday, and... I just want to leave." When he doesn't respond, I add, "Please."

"*Please,*" Tanner repeats, mockery dripping from his voice. "*Please, Tanner, just drop the biggest fucking job you've ever had because I'm scared.*"

Hurt and confusion shudder through me at his words. This isn't like him at all. He's never been mean to me, never disrespected me like this before. I plant my hands on his chest and push away from him, but his arms are looped around me in a vice grip, and all my efforts get me nowhere.

"Let go of me," I plead, hating how small my voice sounds. It's a stark reminder of how much bigger than me Tanner is. Before, I've always found the way his frame towers over mine to be mouthwatering. But now, I'm starting to realize that he's a lot stronger than me, and that thought quickly sours into fear as I begin to struggle against him in earnest.

"Now why would I do that, Bailey?" he sneers. His eyes are cold, betraying no trace of the man I know. His grip on me is crushing, and no amount of thrashing seems to make a difference.

"Tanner, please, you're hurting me!" I cry.

Ignoring my protests, he tightens his arms around me even further before picking me up and tossing me easily onto the bed. Air rushes from my lungs as my back hits the mattress. I struggle to catch my breath while Tanner advances on me, his eyes hungry.

"We're not leaving," he snarls. "You're mine."

The phrase isn't a new one. How many times has that tumbled from his lips in the throes of passion? But it had been a promise then, not a threat. The way he says it now, laced with poison and possession, injects icy fear into my veins.

Tears stream down my face as Tanner looms over me, staring at me with feverish intensity. I struggle to sit up. I need to get away from him. This isn't the man I love. Something's happened to him to make him like this, I'm sure of it. Whoever is standing in front of me, it's no longer Tanner.

I won't let my mind fill in the rest of that thought.

I manage to stand as he grabs me again, this time gripping me hard by the upper arms. Before I can react, he crushes his lips against mine in a painful kiss.

Terror urges me to catch his bottom lip with my teeth and bite down hard.

"You little bitch!" he roars, pushing me away from him. Blood runs down his chin, and in that moment, he no longer looks human. He rushes toward me, and without even thinking, I ball up my fingers against my palm and swing my arm with as much force as I can muster.

My fist connects squarely with his left eye. The noise is wet and sickening, sending a roll of nausea cramping through my stomach. Pain blossoms in my knuckles and wrist as Tanner reels backward, howling like a wounded animal as his hands fly up to claw at his face.

I don't wait to see what he does next. Instead, I dart out of the room toward the front door. I'm somehow still holding my phone from earlier in my left hand, and I grab my purse and keys on the way out. I can hear Tanner behind me, crashing around in the bedroom, but I don't stop, not even to put on my shoes.

Barefoot and cradling my throbbing hand, I let my panic carry me to my car. I gasp from the pain in my injured limb as I struggle to turn the key in the ignition. Part of me braces for the engine to stall or for that fucking song to blast over the radio, but neither of those things happen. The vehicle starts with ease, and the only music that greets me is the peppy beat of a pop song.

A sob of relief escapes me as I back out of the driveway and pull onto the street. I don't look back until I'm halfway down the road. One glance in the rearview mirror fills my heart with horror.

Tanner, blood streaming from his lacerated lip and covered in bruises, is standing in the driveway, glaring at me with fathomless eyes as I speed away from him.

But I know that's not Tanner, not really.

Not anymore.

20

————————

## MEMORIES GONE

Tanner

WHAT THE FUCK happened last night?

I'm lying in bed–alone. There's a terrible taste in my mouth, like I've been sucking up swamp water through a straw. My head is pounding, and when I try to open my eyes, my left lid won't budge. Every muscle in my body aches as though I went toe-to-toe with a semi-truck and lost.

Groaning, I roll out of bed in spite of my body's protests. I'm so thirsty. All I can think of is downing a nice, cool glass of water.

I stumble into the bathroom, half-blind, and after one glance in the mirror, it's immediately apparent why I can't see properly. One of my eyes is bruised and blackened, the lid entirely swollen shut. When I press my fingertips to my cheekbone, I wince in pain.

"What the fuck?" I mutter, squinting at my reflection. The shiner isn't the only injury I have. There's blood caked around my mouth and down my chin, and my lip is split. Below that, mottled purple bruises creep over the skin of my neck and collarbone.

I feel like I've been in a fight, but I can't remember a goddamn thing.

Gripping the sides of the sink, I stare myself down as I try to recall what happened. I have a clear memory of working at the house, of going out to my truck to get a respirator, but everything after that is black velvet, fuzzy and bottomless.

God, I'm so thirsty. It's like I haven't drank in days. Not even bothering to find a glass, I turn on the tap and cup my hands under the water. The clear liquid pools in my palms, and I gulp it down greedily.

When I've had my fill, I splash the cool water up onto my face, watching as the crusted blood flakes off into the basin. My lip stings where the skin is split. How did it happen? The gap in my memory is unsettling, and I've got a dreadful feeling that I did something horrible during that time.

Once my face is clean, I shuck off my clothes. Everything smells like the marsh, cloying and fetid. Dry, crumbling mud cakes the bottoms of my jeans up to the knee. My boots are in no better shape. I'm going to have to hose them down in the driveway to get them any semblance of clean.

I finish stripping down and then step into the shower. The hot water stings against the bruises on my neck and face. I've certainly taken my fair share of punches throughout my life, and I'm pretty sure that the shiner is a direct result of somebody's fist getting friendly with my eye. Had they somehow hit me hard enough to give me a concussion or something? Maybe that would explain the other injuries and the lost time.

It doesn't hit me until I'm out of the shower that I woke up alone.

Where is Bailey?

Worry gnaws at me as I peer out into the bedroom. The bed is unmade. Bailey's charge is plugged into the wall, but her phone is gone. There's no sign of her, even though the daylight streaming through the windows tell me that she should be home from her night shift by now.

Had something happened to her too?

"Babe?" I call, hoping that she's simply in another room. But there's no response.

I finish drying off and throw on the first clean clothes I can find. Wearing jeans and an old T-shirt, I poke around, looking for my phone so I can call her. As I search, I try to convince myself that she's probably stepped out to do some errands or to grab a coffee

After tearing apart the house looking for my phone, I finally think to check my truck. Sure enough, it's sitting on the passenger seat.

Relief floods through me but is quickly staunched when I unlock my phone to see several missed messages, including one from Bailey.

*Where are you? Are you okay?*

It says it's from yesterday.

My heart drops as I double check today's date on the device's calendar.

"A whole day?" I breathe in disbelief. "How can I be missing an entire day?"

Bailey must be so fucking worried about me. Almost automatically, I dial her number. The line rings and rings, and then finally her voice chirps that she's not able to make it to the phone right now and to leave a message after the beep.

"Come on, pick up," I urge as I click on the name again. But the result is the same.

Desperation building inside of me, I tap out a text to her and send it immediately.

*Where are you babe? Answer your phone please. I'm worried.*

Almost immediately, a ping alerts me to a reply.

*This is Bailey's mom. I know what you did to her. Don't contact her again, or I'll go to the police.*

"What the fuck?" I exclaim. A tremor of fear slices through me at the words. Could I have done something to harm Bailey? Had I scared her? Is she okay?

Panicked thoughts swirl through my brain as I try to figure out what to do next. My first instinct is to drive to Bailey's mom's house and get some answers, but the text indicates that they'll probably call the cops the moment they see my truck pull up in the driveway.

Unsure of what to do, I scroll through my other messages to see if there are any clues to help me understand my missing time. One from Jose piques my interest. Yesterday morning, he had texted several times to ask if I was going to come to the job site or if I was sick. It was easy to conclude that I hadn't made it to work that day.

With no other avenues to consider, I decide the most practical thing I can do is retrace my steps starting with the last thing I can remember.

That strategy means going back to the house. After all, looking for the spare respirator in my truck was the last thing I can recall before the missing time. Maybe I'll find some answers back at the job site?

I waste no time driving over to the old Gregory place. Navigating with only one working eye proves to be a bit tricky, but I manage to pull up the old cypress-lined drive with no major problems.

The house, silent and empty, stares down at me as I step out onto the gravel. Insects sing a riotous chorus in the swamp beyond, which is wreathed in a greenish haze beneath the midday sun. The air is heavy with humidity. I can already feel beads of sweat gathering on my forehead and between my shoulder blades.

For a moment, I'm confused why there's nobody here working, but then I realize that it's Saturday today. The vacant job site only bolsters my unease that I can't remember an entire day of my life.

Steeling myself for whatever I may find, I enter the house. I remember that I had been working on the section of drywall in the kitchen, but I hadn't started working on the wall because I couldn't find my respirator. Therefore, the kitchen is the best place to start.

But when I make my way to the room in question, I'm puzzled to find that the wall has already been neatly removed. Did I do that, or did my crew take care of it? I eye the sheets of fresh drywall leaning against the kitchen counter, which is covered with a drop cloth.

Nothing in here is sparking any memories. The gaping hole in the studs I meant to fix remains.

I'm even more confused now than I was when I woke up this morning. Troubled thoughts needle my mind as I head back outside to examine the driveway. But that search turns out to be fruitless, too.

By the time I've scoured every inch of the gravel, I'm ready to give up. I sigh and slump against the side of my truck, tilting my face up to meet the blistering summer sun.

"Rough night?" a smooth, serpentine voice asks from beside me.

Startled, I whip around to face the speaker. A figure, more familiar than I'd care to admit, stands next to me, casually leaning against the truck. A shard of a memory flashes back to me—this person, this *thing*, grinning at me in the kitchen.

"You," I hiss.

The thing smiles. It's a wonder that I ever mistook it for Dalton, or even for a human being, in the first place. In the bright light of day, it looks almost faded. Its ashen face is shadowed in spite of the sun overhead. It looks like a wax figure brought to life, too uncanny to possibly be real.

"Call me Amos," it insists, its tone dripping with false politeness. "Since we're so close."

"Did you do this to me?" I demand, gesturing to the marks on my neck and face.

Amos chuckles. "Don't you remember?"

I ball my hands into fists, fuming. "No," I say through gritted teeth. "I don't."

"I do," it grins, revealing yellowed, pointed teeth. "We had a lot of fun yesterday, you and I. Bailey didn't seem too keen, though."

Anger surges through me at the mention of the woman I love. My mind snaps back to her mother's text, demanding I leave Bailey alone. Had I hurt her? Had *Amos* hurt her?

"What did you do?" I snarl.

"Not enough," it laments. "But I'll fix that soon."

"No, you won't," I assure it, my fingers balling into fists at my sides.

Amos laughs again, and I struggle against the urge to clamp my hands to my ears at the sound. "One way or another, Bailey will be mine."

"Like hell she will!"

The thing steps forward until its face is only inches from mine. When it speaks, putrid breath fans across my face. "You think you can stand against me?" it challenges. "Better men have tried and failed. Now they're rotting at the bottom of the swamp."

I'm seething with rage, too angry to even reply. All I know is that even if I'm doomed, I will not let this thing have Bailey. I love her, more than anything. I won't let him have her. Not while I'm alive.

"She's mine," I growl. "She will always be mine."

"We'll see about that," Amos smirks.

The dam inside me bursts. Without conscious thought, a roar of anger erupts from my throat. I swing my fist at the thing, longing to feel its waxy, unnatural skin split beneath my knuckles.

But my fist sails only through air.

The thing is gone.

I stagger forward a few steps before regaining my balance.

"Show yourself, you fucking coward!" I howl toward the swamp.

But nothing moves.

The only indication that Amos was ever there at all is the grating, horrible laugh that drifts through the cypress trees and fizzles out beneath the blistering summer sun.

21

———————

# LURED

Bailey

HOW DID *everything spiral so far out of control?*

I ask myself that question for the thousandth time, but I still don't have a good answer.

At least I can lose myself in my work. After rotting in bed over the weekend, I'm relieved to escape my childhood home and my mom's knowing, silent stare. I don't have any of my scrubs with me, but I'm able to track down a clean change of clothes packed away in a box in my old closet. My shoes are presumably still sitting in the hallway of the house I'd fled. I wasn't about to go back to retrieve them, so I've settled on wearing a pair of borrowed flip flops.

One glance in the mirror reveals that I look more like I'm going to some backyard barbecue than a nursing night shift. Shame washes over me at the sight of my reflection. Professionalism has always been very important to me. I guess that's just one more way in which I've failed.

My mom gives me a tight hug before I head out, promising to have some food ready for me when I come back early the next morning.

And then I'm sitting in the car, alone again, as I drive to the Wilsons' house on the edge of the swamp. I pass by the shaded path to the old Gregory place on the way, but I keep my eyes fixed forward on the road ahead. Even so, I can't help but wonder if Tanner, or the thing that isn't Dalton, is there right now.

Or maybe they both are.

The thought chills me to the bone.

Shaking the feeling away, I try to prepare myself to act normal in front of the Wilsons. I have no doubts that my mom's probably already called Helen, since they are close friends, and apprised her of the situation.

I dread to think what she might have told the Wilsons. I know my mother thinks that Tanner did this to me, that we'd had a fight that had gotten out of hand. She quizzed me over and over, but I kept my mouth shut, even when she drove me to the nearest urgent care to get my hand X-rayed.

How am I supposed to explain to her that I think an entity is possessing the man I love and made him attack me?

No, I'm better off saying nothing at all.

Helen is waiting for me on the front porch when I pull into the driveway of the Wilson home. Her features are creased with worry, dismal confirmation that my mom has already told the older woman everything.

"Hey, honey," she greets me as I step out of my vehicle into the humid evening air. "How are you? Your momma told me you're not feeling so great."

I'm sure my mother told her a lot more than that, but I bite back the sassy comment and instead plaster a smile on my face, hoping it looks more cheerful than I feel. "Oh, you know how she is, always exaggerating," I say, waving my hand in the air as though I can brush the comments away. "I'm fine, really."

The older woman doesn't seem convinced, especially when her eyes land on my injured, bandaged hand and narrow suspiciously. Dread pools in my gut as I wait for her to ask if Tanner was responsible for my pitiful state, but she subverts my expectations and instead breezes, "Well, let's not stand out here in the heat. I've got the AC on. Come on in."

She ushers me inside the house and out of the dusky driveway. I'm glad to be indoors. I don't think I could stand being outside in the dark this close to the swamp. A shiver runs through me as I imagine a figure moving out there in the shadows of the cypress trees, slithering over the tangled roots and jagged gravestones fighting for space in the mire.

"Robert's taking a nap," Helen tells me as she leads me upstairs. "He's been sleeping so poorly."

"Even with the change in medication?" I ask, falling easily into my professional role. Discussing work is easy and comfortable, a welcome respite from the troubled thoughts that snarl through my mind.

Helen nods. "Actually, I think it's gotten worse," she admits. "He used to be able to get a few hours until the drugs wore off, but now he's up every hour or so. Sometimes he talks in his sleep, but I can't make sense of anything he says."

"I'll see what I can do for him tonight, and then I'll call his doctor first thing tomorrow morning," I assure her.

In spite of his insomnia, Robert is sound asleep when we reach the bedroom. I run down my checklist, noting his vitals and caring for the wound. Helen watches in silence as I gingerly clean around the healing skin before I dress his leg with fresh bandages. He's not due for more medication for a few more hours, but I prep the supplies anyway.

Finally, when there is nothing else left for me to do, Helen and I retreat to the kitchen for a cup of coffee.

As she places a mug down on the table in front of me, Helen gestures to my bandaged arm. "You must be relieved it's not broken," she says. Her tone is careful, as though she's worried she'll spook me.

I nod in response.

She purses her lips as she slides into the seat across from me and folds her hands around her own cup of coffee. "Tanner didn't do it." It's not a question. Unease glints in her eyes.

"No," I reply slowly, holding her gaze. "He didn't. At least...I don't think so."

A sigh escapes the older woman as she shakes her head. "I was worried about this," she murmurs, her eyes flicking down to the swirling depths of the coffee mug nestled between her palms. "I thought that maybe with the house being gone..."

"What?" I urge, fear surging through me. "What do you know?"

Helen's gaze meets mine again, and I'm surprised to see tears welling there. "I grew up in this house," she breathes in a shaky whisper, barely audible above the gentle hum of the refrigerator. "One night, when I was a little girl, I stayed up late. It was a small act of rebellion, but I was always such a golden child. It was simply thrilling." She turns her head to stare out the darkened window toward the swamp. "I was up in my bedroom, the room Robert's in now. I had gotten this sense that I *needed* to look out the window, like my life depended on it. So I looked. At first I only saw darkness. But then, when I turned my attention out toward the Gregory house, I saw..."

"A man." I finish for her. "A man that isn't a man."

Understanding settles between us, and she nods. "You've seen him too." Once again, it's not a question. "Back then, I thought my mind must be playing tricks on me. But I saw him again, and again, and again, until one day, I decided to investigate. One night, I snuck out the back door and waited at the edge of the marsh. Sure enough, he appeared over by the old cemetery. Every bone in my body screamed that I shouldn't go any farther, but a part of me had to know who this man was. And so I waded into the swamp. But every time I got close, he would dance farther away, just out of reach. Before I knew it, I was chest deep in the mud, water closing in around me. It dawned on me then that I was in terrible danger, but I had gone too far."

"It lured you in," I gasp.

"It did," she confirms somberly. "And it would have kept me there—except that my father had heard the door slam behind me when I snuck out. He came in after me and pulled me out. And the whole time, that thing *laughed.*"

Ice curls down my spine. I try to imagine being trapped in the mire, the putrid murk sloughing in around me. The stench that had clung to Tanner the night he grabbed me fills my nostrils, and it takes everything in me not to gag at the memory.

"Miraculously, I was okay," Helen continues. Her eyes are glassy, lost in a time long past. "I was filthy, of course. And my father, who had never raised his voice to anybody, shouted at me to never, ever go into the swamp again, especially after dark."

Silence falls in the kitchen as her story concludes. It takes me a moment to find my voice, but when I do, I ask, "Did your father tell you what it is?"

She shakes her head ruefully. "No," she sighs. "He said it was against God. But that's not to say I never found out. My nanny knew the truth. She told me what my father couldn't. That thing out there is older than any of us. It was here when her grandmother had worked the land, and even she had grown up with the stories. They have a name for it." She pauses and draws in a deep, shuddering breath. "Asmodeus."

Something clicks inside of me as forgotten Sunday school lessons and old local legends fall into place. "A demon," I whisper through my mounting dread.

Helen looks as sick as I feel. "My nanny said her grandmother had helped bind this demon to the Gregory family. They thought that by doing so, the entity could be controlled. But there was a price to pay, a steep price. Every Gregory who has lived in that house has paid since then."

"Layla," I realize.

"I don't think it was a coincidence that the house burned down," Helen says. She must not know that Penny set the fire, and I don't tell her now. "I think Layla came face to face with Asmodeus. I had hoped that the fire would cleanse the property of the evil, but I fear that while it may have weakened the demon, perhaps it also freed it to prey on more than just the Gregory family."

Horrified, I utter, "And now it's got Tanner."

It's clear that Helen's fears have been realized as I put the pieces together. "Tanner didn't do that to you, Bailey," she tells me, pointing toward my injured wrist. "Asmodeus did."

At her words, my world comes crashing down. Bile rises in my throat as I wrestle with the terrible certainty that I'm not crazy, that all of these horrible things that have happened are real. After a moment, I choke out, "What do I do?"

"Wait here," the older woman instructs. She rises from her seat and strides quickly out of the room, leaving me alone at the kitchen table. Fear, acid and irrational, bubbles up inside of me at her absence. I swear I can feel eyes burning into me, but I refuse to look toward the window overlooking the swamp. Just as I decide that I can't possibly bear it any longer, Helen returns.

"Here."

She places a yellowed, ragged piece of paper onto the table in front of me. It looks old, and it's creased in a way that tells me it's been folded and unfolded dozens of times.

"What is it?" I ask, squinting down at the words. It's a language I don't recognize, like a mix of French, English, and something else entirely.

"It's a Voodoo spell," Helen explains. "My nanny's grandmother was a priestess, and that gift was passed down through the generations. She told me that if I were to ever encounter the demon again, that this incantation would destroy it. I memorized it as a little girl, and I still know it by heart to this very day."

I stare down at the scrawled writing.

Would this really be enough to kill a demon?

There was only one way to find out.

22

———————————

## GHOST STORIES

Tanner

NEVER IN MY life have I felt so wretched.

I'm slumped down in a chair at Hahnville's only café, nursing a cup of coffee. I've been here for an hour. Bailey is set to arrive any minute, but I wanted the time to prepare myself before she shows up. Just the fact that she's agreed to meet me here sends my heart racing.

What am I supposed to tell her? The truth is unbelievable, but I don't have any other explanation. My memories of the past few days are spotty and fractured. The pieces I do recall are cloudy and dream-like. The only thing I'm sure of is that I hurt Bailey, and that is unforgivable.

Leaning my head back and closing my eyes, I try desperately to clear my foggy mind. My whole body aches. The blackened flesh around my left eye is still swollen and has now curdled toward a greenish tinge. The angry bruises that ring my neck aren't faring much better. I know I look like shit. People have been shooting me curious glances all weekend, and I wonder if they suspect that I might have done something terrible to my girlfriend.

I sigh and take a sip of my coffee. It's long since gone cold, but I barely taste it as I swallow a mouthful. All I can think about is Bailey.

*Speak of the devil.*

The door to the café opens, and there she is, hesitating on the threshold as she scans the tables until her eyes fall on me.

I look away quickly. I can't bear to see the disgust that I know must be on Bailey's face as she catches sight of me. It isn't until I hear the chair across from me scrape against the floor that I dare to meet her gaze.

"Tanner?" she asks quietly, as though she needs confirmation that it's really me. Her voice is small and tentative, her eyes heavy with trepidation.

"Yeah," I croak out in reply. Whatever caused the bruising on my neck did a number on my voice as well.

Her small body sags with relief at my words.

Guilt swirls in my gut as I watch her carefully. She's clearly had a hard time the last few days. Dark smudges beneath her eyes tell me that she hasn't been sleeping well, and her skin is pale and waxy as though she's been ill. Her hair, usually brushed and glossy, is knotted in a messy bun on top of her head. She's wearing old clothes and a pair of flip flops that are comically large on her.

But the worst part is her right arm. Bandages wrap tightly around her hand and wrist. Her exposed knuckles are puffy and bruised. Even though I can't remember it, I'm suddenly sure that I did that to her.

"Oh god," I breathe. My eyes are glued to her injured arm. "I'm sorry, baby. I'm so, so sorry."

Bailey shakes her head. "Do you remember?" she asks.

I close my eyes in an attempt to hold back the tears that collect there. "I don't," I whisper. "But it was me, wasn't it?"

"Not exactly," she replies. Surprise floods through me as I feel the fingers of her uninjured hand intertwine with mine.

My eyes snap open. "What do you mean?"

She bites her lip, clearly unsure of where to start. Finally, she posits, "What do you know about demons?"

"Demons?" I repeat.

"Do you remember the stories we used to tell as kids?" she continues, pushing forward in spite of my confusion. "About the swamp being haunted?"

I nod. Even though we hadn't grown up together, I'm pretty sure that we both had gotten the same tired ghost stories passed around in the hallways about such places around our hometowns.

"I know this sounds crazy, but what if the stories are true?" Her tone is fervent, and her eyes shine with a hot certainty. "Not the witches and stuff. But there is something there, and I think..." She draws in a deep, steadying breath. "I think it's a demon."

"Amos," I murmur. I'm not entirely sure where the name comes from, but it pops out from my subconscious amidst a cloud of dread.

"Oh my god," Bailey gasps. Fear flashes across her face. "That's the name Miss Penny would say all the time. Amos...Asmodeus. What if they're the same thing?"

I really don't understand what she's talking about. My head begins to pound at the mention of the names. Blood pulses painfully behind my left eye. All I want to do is bury my head in my hands and feel sorry for myself, but I also know this is my one chance to make it right with Bailey. I'm not going to fuck it up.

"You said it wasn't exactly me," I press, changing the subject. "What does that even mean?"

Bailey scrutinizes me for a long moment. Just when my patience is about to snap, she blurts out, "I think the demon was possessing you."

Time stops.

Part of me wants to laugh in her face. Here I am, sitting across from the woman I so clearly battered, hoping for any explanation that will absolve me of my sins. I'm not sure what I was expecting, but it certainly wasn't demons. No, I wouldn't use that as a cop-out.

Even though I don't remember them, I've always prided myself in being the type of person who takes responsibility for my actions.

But even as I struggle to rationalize Bailey's words, bitter understanding congeals in my gut. Somewhere, deep underneath reason and sanity, I know that what she's saying is true.

An image of a cruel, pointed grin flashes through my mind, and I wince.

"Are you okay?" Bailey asks, her tone laced with concern.

I nod through the sudden pain. Blinking away the horrible image, I request, "Tell me what happened." When Bailey hesitates, I beg, "Please, I need to know. Please."

Agony weaves through her features before she bows her head, shielding her expression from my questioning gaze. My stomach turns. What is so bad that she doesn't even want to face me?

"I... I don't know all of it," she begins. "Only what happened on Friday. I got home from my shift at the Wilsons', but you weren't there. When I realized that you probably hadn't been home since the day before, I was really worried. I hoped you might have called or texted, but there was nothing, and you weren't even answering your phone. While I was waiting to hear back from you, I fell asleep."

She pauses, and I know her well enough to conclude that she's trying to hold back her tears.

"Did I come home?" I probe, urging her to continue.

She nods, and when she speaks again, her voice sounds haunted. "You were just standing there in the doorway, watching me sleep. It was... creepy. I knew something wasn't right. And you looked terrible, Tanner. Like, somebody had beaten you up or something."

"This?" I ask, gesturing to my black eye.

"No." She still doesn't meet my gaze. "That came later." She lets out an unsteady breath before resuming her narrative. "There were bruises on your neck. It looked like... like somebody had tried to strangle you. But you wouldn't tell me who did it. You weren't making any sense; it was like you were a different person. It wasn't you."

Thunder rolls through my head. Fragments of quasi-memories flash across my mind. Sunlight in the bedroom. Bailey sprawled on the bed, fear in her eyes. Oh god. What had I done to her?

Bailey pushes forward. "You... said some things. And I told you I thought we should get out of town. You didn't like that. You pushed me down onto the bed and you... you tried to...."

Her voice drifts off into silence between us. Shame wells inside me as bile rises in my throat. I don't want to hear anymore. I don't want to know.

"I got away." The words do little to quench my self-loathing. "I... I bit you, and then punched you. That's how you got the black eye, I guess."

It certainly does explain some things, though I still have no idea where the bruises on my neck came from. Desperately desiring to steer the conversation away from what I came dangerously close to doing, I ask, "Your hand... is it broken?"

"Just sprained," she informs me. It's a small mercy, but not enough to chip away at my devastating guilt. She catches my hand again, and I drag my eyes up to meet hers. Her expression is fierce, protective. "We need to get out of here, Tanner. This thing is destroying us."

Rage surges through me, and I struggle to tamp it down. I don't even know why I'm so angry at the suggestion of leaving town. "One more day," I counter. It's the only compromise I can think of. Hopefully, it's enough to swallow down the rabid emotions that threaten to consume me. "Just one more day, and the house will be done."

"It isn't worth it, Tanner," she argues. "The money isn't worth our lives."

"I'm so close." I hate the pleading edge in my voice. I sound like an addict asking for one more fix before I quit. And yet I continue to wheedle, "All I need to do is repair one thing in the kitchen. The guys can take care of the rest. Just give me tomorrow. Please, Bailey. One more day?"

Arguments flit across her face as she struggles to counter my request. But then she sags down in her chair, the fight leaving her. "Fine," she capitulates. "One more day, but then I'm leaving–with or without you.

The thought of her abandoning me here to the mercy of the thing in the swamp is unbearable.

"I promise." I lift her uninjured hand to my mouth and press my lips gently against the soft skin of her palm. She sighs at the attention, her eyelids fluttering closed.

I lean in to kiss her, longing to feel her body melt against mine. But she stands abruptly before I can move closer, breaking our proximity.

Clearing her throat awkwardly, she says, "I have to go. Call me as soon as you're done tomorrow."

"I will," I swear to her. My nerves burn with desire for her, but I know I have to let her go. Part of her is still afraid of me, even if she believes that I was possessed by a demon at the time I'd hurt her.

Regret wells in me as I watch her retreat. I should have apologized to her. I should have told her I love her. But it's too late now.

I sit for a while after Bailey leaves.

*One more day.*

All I need to do is fix the drywall in the kitchen, and then Jose can guide the crew through the rest. I'll tell Jake that I have to leave town for a family emergency. We can do it. We can get away from this.

I drop some cash on the table and exit the café. I grimace as I step out into the cloying afternoon heat, a stark contrast to the crisp air conditioning I've just left. Even in spite of the oppressive weather, I can't help but feel hopeful for the future.

But as I pass by the wide glazed windows of the storefront, I catch a glimpse of my reflection.

Amos smirks back at me from the glass.

"No!" I groan, clapping my hands to my temples as pain rips through my head. I can feel him in there, clawing at the shadows of my mind while his laugh scuttles around inside my skull.

When I collapse onto the sunbaked concrete of the sidewalk, the silence comes as a sweet relief.

*One more day.*

Can I last that long?

# 23

# SHARED EXPERIENCE

Bailey

I FEEL POWERLESS.

Anxiety gnaws at me as I lie in bed, my mind playing back the agreement that Tanner and I had brokered yesterday afternoon. I'd given him one last day to sort out the situation at the construction site. Keeping my side of the deal, I'd told Helen at the beginning of my shift that we were leaving town. The older woman had been supportive and understanding, urging me to do whatever I needed to do to get away from the swamp.

Now all I have to do is wait for Tanner's workday to finish later this evening, and we'll be free.

But it's torturous, sitting here unable to do anything. I've already packed myself a bag and taken some money out of the bank. Other than that, I can't think of anything else that I can possibly do to prepare, especially since we don't even know where we're going once we leave.

Tanner has a large family spread out all over the country. Maybe we'd be able to stay with a cousin or an aunt for a while until we can find somewhere to settle. Or perhaps we could head to Florida and seek out Layla, who would surely help us once she knows what we've been going through.

I should call her, I decide. It will give me something to do to kill the time, especially since my mind's been cooking up horrible scenarios of the demon forcing Tanner to do unforgivable things.

Rolling out of bed, I pad over to the door of my childhood room and ease it shut. It's still very early, and I don't want to wake my mom up. I've already told her that I'm going to go away for a while to clear my head, and she had agreed that it was a healthy idea. I think she might change her mind if she heard me rambling about demons and curses.

I settle back down on the bed and pull out my phone, dialing Layla's number before I have the chance to chicken out. The phone rings once, and then she picks up.

"Hey girl!" Layla greets me.

A dam inside me breaks at the sound of my friend's voice, and the tears I've been holding back since yesterday burst out in a deep, wretched sob.

"Bailey?" Layla asks, her tone more urgent now. "Sweetie, what's wrong?"

"We're leaving," I choke out between shaking breaths. "We're getting out of this fucking place. I can't stand this any longer, I can't, I..."

"Whoa, Bailey. Slow down," she soothes. "What's happened? Are you okay?"

I draw in a shuddering gulp of air, trying to calm myself down. Finally, I'm collected enough to whisper, "I'm scared, Layla."

There's a pause before she presses, "What's going on, Bailey? Talk to me."

"There's something in the swamp," I babble. "Something evil. It...it wants Tanner."

Silence crawls down the line. It stretches on for so long that I'm starting to think that my service has dropped when Layla whispers, "Amos."

The name drips with dread and hangs between us like a dead thing.

"He came for you, too," I utter. Even though I've always suspected, I know it for sure now.

Layla sniffles, and I realize she's crying. "He did," she admits finally. "He started fucking with me the moment I stepped foot in Aunt Penny's house."

I close my eyes and wait in horrified stillness for her to speak again.

After a long moment, she continues, "Everything I know is kind of pieced together. From what I understand, the demon's always been there, wandering out in the swamp. Ages ago, my ancestors made some kind of deal with it, but it went wrong. It's been haunting the property ever since, driving the Gregory family crazy and killing anybody who gets too close."

"Helen said it's called Asmodeus," I add. "They used some kind of voodoo spell." It sounds so wild when I say it out loud. Do I really believe in witchcraft and conjuring and all of that woo-woo nonsense?

*Yes.* After all the things I've seen, I have no doubt in my mind.

"I swear, Bailey, I thought it was gone." Layla sounds sick to her stomach. "But I should have realized. I should have warned you. And when you told me that Tanner was working there, I...I fucked up. I failed you."

"No," I tell her firmly. "None of this is your fault. And do you really think I would have believed you if you had told me right away? It's undeniable now that I've seen it with my own eyes, but back then, I would have thought you'd lost your mind."

"It really is back, isn't it?" Layla whispers.

"It is," I confirm. "But I need to know. What happened to you there?"

Layla sighs. "It tried to take me, to use my like it used Aunt

Penny. It started small. I'd have these weird dreams. I'd lose time. Objects would move around or appear from nowhere. Roses," she remembers in a haunted tone. "It would leave me roses."

"Did you ever see it?" I ask, thinking back to the thing that wasn't Dalton that had hunted me in my bedroom.

"Yeah, out in the swamp. I followed it once. Dalton had to pull me out of the mud. And I felt it. Remember the time we all went to the club in NOLA?"

A shudder runs through me as I recall the hands that had roamed my body and the horrible things the demon has hissed into my ear at the same bar. "Yeah," I say. "Why?"

"It followed me there," Layla explains. "I'd had a bit too much to drink, and I was dancing, and I... I thought it was Dalton. It kind of looked like him. But it wasn't. I think... I think that was the first time I really understood that something bad was happening."

"I saw it there too," I confess, squeezing my eyes shut against the onslaught of emotion. "It... touched me. That's why I asked about Dalton last time we talked. It had looked like Tanner at first, and then like Dalton. I guess I thought it would be better to chalk it up to your boyfriend having a wild night out than a demon coming after me in a club."

We sit for a moment as we both try to process what we've heard. Every revelation is more horrifying than the last, but it's also strangely cathartic to let the truth out to somebody who understands unconditionally.

Layla is the first to break the silence. "You said it wants Tanner?" she asks.

"I know it sounds crazy, but I think it possessed him," I say. "He lost time, said he didn't remember anything. He tried to... he grabbed me. I punched him and got away. It was his body, but it wasn't him inside. I know it wasn't."

"Oh god," Layla gasps. "Bailey, I'm so sorry. Are you okay?"

"I'm fine," I lie, staring down at my swollen, bandaged hand. "I gave him a pretty good shiner though."

"It took Dalton, too, right before the fire," my friend tells me. "It used him to try to get to me. I think... maybe it doesn't want Tanner. Maybe it wants you, and he's just a tool to get you."

Bile rises in my throat at the thought. This whole time, I'd assumed that the demon wanted Tanner. Given the amount of time he'd been spending out at the old Gregory property, I'd just thought that he'd have been the easiest target and that I was just collateral.

Is it possible that Amos has been after me the whole time?

I think back to how its body had pressed against mine in the club. At the time, I'd been into it, thinking it was Tanner. But now....

Desperately needing to change the subject, I pivot and ask, "What really happened with the fire?"

"Aunt Penny started it on purpose," she confirms. "She knew that Amos was getting too strong. It was the only thing she could do to try to stop it. After you helped me get her out, Amos took over Dalton to try to claim me before the house burned down. We just barely got away. Honestly, it's a miracle we're both still alive."

She isn't exaggerating. The sight of the old Gregory home in flames had frightened me more than anything in my life up until that point. Even Tanner, who had been there fighting back the scorching tongues of the fire, had been shocked that all of us had made it out relatively unscathed. Demons aside, they had been very lucky.

Layla adds, "Before she died, Aunt Penny and I made a pact that no Gregory would ever set foot on the property again. We'd hoped that after the fire, Amos had been killed or banished or whatever happens to demons when they go away for good. But maybe it just weakened it."

"What if the fire freed it?" I pose, echoing what Helen had said to me a few nights before. "What if its power was weakened, but the curse that bound it to the Gregory family was broken?"

Horror blossoms between us as we ponder the consequences of the theory. It makes sense, especially if the demon is after me now that Layla's out of the picture. Did that mean it was still attached to the property? Maybe it could only follow us temporarily, but that connection would be broken by time and distance?

I had to believe we could run far and fast–and ultimately be free.

"We're leaving tonight," I tell her.

"Where will you go?"

"Anywhere, as long as it's not here," I reply staunchly.

"Come to Florida," Layla offers, her tone pleading. "You can stay with us as long as you need to. We can help you find a place. Dalton can find some work for Tanner, and I think you'd be a great fit if you want to join my team for a while."

It's such a tempting offer. Even though I really don't want to refuse, I double check, "Are you sure? What if it tries to follow us?"

"Then we'll fuck it up for good," she says fiercely. "It'll be four against one."

"Okay," I breathe over the phone. I can already imagine Tanner and I packed into his truck, rolling down the highway toward the state line out of Louisiana. Sweet relief teases my nerves as I let myself bask in the possibilities of freedom. "As soon as Tanner's done, we'll head your way."

Layla sucks in a sharp gasp. "Done? Done with what?" she asks, her tone urgent once again.

"He's just getting everything sorted at the construction site so we can leave," I explain.

My friend's voice rises in alarm. "The construction site? As in, Aunt Penny's place?"

Dread swirls through me as I realize where Layla is going with this. "Yeah," I say weakly.

"Bailey, listen to me. If Tanner is at the house, you need to go get him. Right fucking now, do you hear me? Get him and go!"

Overwhelmed by sour fear, I have to admit that she's right.

I have to go to the house.

I have to face the demon.

Tanner's life might depend on it.

# 24

# CACKLING DEMON

Tanner

"TANNER?"

I stare at the hole in the drywall. It gapes open like the maw of some unknowable beast, just waiting to devour anybody unwitting enough to step into its jaws.

*What would it feel like to watch this house consume somebody?*

Hungry desire washes through me at the thought. My hands clench into tight fists at my sides, my nails digging into the calloused skin of my palms.

"Tanner!"

Fingers close on my shoulder, and I whip around, my heart beating wildly.

"Take it easy, boss," Jose placates, taking a step back from me and holding his hands up as if to show me that he means me no harm.

I blink. Of course, it's just my foreman. Who else would it be?

"What?" I growl, hoping my aggressiveness will hide my embarrassment at being caught spacing out like that.

Jose raises an eyebrow but ignores my antagonistic tone. Instead, he asks, "Do you want an extra pair of hands in here?" He nods to the gap in the drywall.

"I've got it," I snap.

"Whatever you say, boss," Jose sighs with a shrug. He gives me one last skeptical look before he retreats from the room.

*Good riddance.*

All I want is to be alone here to do my fucking work.

But there's something about this special space in the drywall, this cut in the skin and flesh of the house rending all the way down to the bone, something that begs me not to cover it.

Not yet.

Shaking my head, I step away from the hole in the wall. "What the fuck's wrong with me?" I mutter.

I haven't felt right since last week. Even yesterday, when I had promised Bailey that I'd finish here today, I'd been hung over and cloudy. I'd passed out on the street in front of the café where we'd met up, and while I remember peeling myself off the sidewalk and stumbling away, I don't recall what had happened after that.

It was as if a split second had passed, and then I had simply found myself here at the old Gregory place, loitering on the edge of the swamp as dawn broke over the stagnant water. The crew had arrived shortly after, and I'd been doing my best since then to pretend that everything is okay.

But it's not.

What had I done in all of that lost time? Would it stop once we got away from this place?

I squeeze my eyes shut. As much as I hate to admit it, I'm not myself, not entirely. Maybe I never will be again.

Pushing that morbid line of thinking away, I grab my measuring tape. I need to mark the fresh sheetrock to make sure it's the proper size to cover the hole.

But before I can even start the task, a harrowing scream rips through the air, drowning out the drone of power tools and idle chatter.

Adrenaline surges through me as I drop the measuring tape and spring into action. As I burst out into the hallway, I see Jose and several of the others doing the same.

"Upstairs!" one of the guys shouts, barely audible over the shrieks echoing off the bare walls.

We move as a pack toward the sound, surging up the stairs in a mass of bodies. I push my way to the front of the group as we reach the landing, where one of the crew, Terry, has been installing balusters for the railing.

Terry's mouth is open in a piercing, continuous wail as he stares down at his hand. Vomit rises in my throat as I realize there's a nail embedded in his palm. It's punctured so deeply that I can see the sharp end sticking out from between the bones and tendons, the metal sandwiching the flesh.

Blood courses down his arm in thick, vibrant veins and spatters in a growing pool beneath him. His face is ashen from pain and shock.

He won't stop screaming.

I know I should go to him and put pressure on his hand to stop the bleeding. I should tell him it'll be fine. I should pull my phone out and call for an ambulance.

But I'm frozen there on the landing, steps away from Terry.

*Let him bleed.*

That horrible voice slides across my thoughts, a serpent in the garden. My eyes are locked onto the man's bloody hand.

The nail glints dully in the midday light.

I can't look away.

People push past me, swarming Terry as I stand rooted to the spot.

"Jesus, man," Jose gasps, gathering his colleague's hand up in a wadded rag. "What the fuck happened?"

One of the guys on the landing pipes up, "We were just getting the balusters in place. The nail gun jammed and when he tried to jimmy it out, it just went off!"

Jose takes a moment to process before he starts barking orders. "Let's get him outside," he commands, securing his arm around Terry's quivering shoulder and guiding the still-screaming man toward the stairs. "Vince, call the hospital and tell them we're bringing him in. He's bleeding too bad for us to wait for an ambulance."

"Sure thing," Vince, the man who had seen the incident, replies.

Satisfied with that answer, Jose turns to me. "Do you want to take him, or should I?" he asks.

I open my mouth to say that Jose should take him so I can control the situation here once the cops come out, but the voice that erupts from my throat isn't my own.

It's that laugh, that terrible, grating fucking *laugh.*

The demon's laugh.

Jose's eyes widen in horror at the sound. Several of the men around me flinch away. Even Terry's scream cuts out.

I clamp my mouth shut, but the damage is already done. Silence rings around us for a moment before the fear on the foreman's face sours to disgust.

"Get out of the fucking way," he spits, checking me with one shoulder so that I have to catch myself against the wall.

Nobody says anything as they close ranks around Terry. Several of the men spare me ugly glances as they file past, ushering him down the stairs, through the hallway, and out into the daylight.

I stay where I am, even as I hear the roar of engines and the slamming of car doors. Soon, the silence tells me that my crew has left, following Jose in a somber procession to the hospital.

"It wasn't me," I moan, sliding down the wall until I'm crumpled on the landing. "It wasn't me."

But there's nobody left to convince.

What is this thing doing to me? I don't want to admit the horrible truth that it's controlling me. Bailey was right. It really is possessing me, pulling my strings and using me like some fucking puppet.

"Fuck you!" I howl to the empty house.

The only reply is the ceaseless buzz of the swamp.

The swamp.

That's where this thing is from, isn't it? Bailey said something about it being connected to the land here. It makes sense. If it was bound to the old Gregory house, it would have turned to ash along with the rest of the place. But it's still here. Weakened, perhaps, but not dead.

It comes from the swamp, and that's where I'll find it.

I struggle to my feet, ignoring the way my head swims as I right myself. Time feels slow as I stumble down the stairs like a drunkard. My limbs are cottony, and my thoughts are thick. All I know is that I need to get to the marsh.

I need to confront this thing, once and for all.

Every step is a struggle. I force myself forward, navigating the hallway until I burst out of the back door and into the fresh air.

I could have sworn that today had been sunny and bright, but now, the sky is gloomy and banked with bruise-colored clouds. Thunder surges in the distance, heralding an oncoming storm. The rank stench of the swamp permeates the oppressive humidity. It's only a matter of time before the rain starts.

"You think a fucking storm will stop me?" I holler at the shadows that dance between the cypress trees. My feet carry me away from the house toward the loamy ground. Insects mutter furiously from amidst the greenish haze that hangs over the water as the tombstones, half-sunken into the mire, beckon me closer.

That's where I'll find it, in the cemetery.

Mud sloshes around me as I wade into the swamp marching toward the graveyard. The water, cloudy with moss and sediment, rushes over my legs. I can feel the gnarled bones of cypress roots beneath my boots, offering me some purchase as I struggle forward.

Finally, I grab a branch and haul myself onto the patch of grass beside one lichen-covered gravestone. I gasp for air, nearly doubled over from the effort it took to climb out here.

A peal of thunder crackles in the distance, and I startle at the sound.

"A little jumpy today, aren't we?" a voice croons from behind me.

I whip around, my fist raised, but the thing that stands before me simply catches my swing with one hand and holds it there with lazy ease.

"Amos," I growl.

How could I have forgotten this thing, even for a second? The shadows of the swamp unmask it for what it really is, something terrible and inhuman. It's still wearing Dalton's face like a disguise, but nothing can hide the evil that lurks beneath.

"At your service," the thing says with a little bow. "Or perhaps it would be more apt to say that you are at mine."

"It's over," I snarl, squaring up to it even as it begins squeezing my fist painfully in its crushing grasp.

"Not quite yet," Amos corrects, grinning. "Did you really think you could simply leave?"

I try to yank my arm back, but it doesn't even budge.

"You shouldn't have come back here," the demon continues as it strengthens its grip on my hand. Pain zips up my wrist and radiates in hot bolts down my arm. "You can't win. The house is almost finished, and then the new woman will be here. She will be mine."

"Then take her," I beg as the agony forces me to my knees. "Take Julia. Just let Bailey go!"

"Now why would I do that?" Amos muses. It regards me as a god would an insect. Is that what it thinks of me? Of people? Are we just toys to it?

"Please," I plead through the blinding pain.

The thing smiles widely. "I don't think I will," it says slowly. "Why choose when I can have both?"

Black spots cluster before my eyes. There's not much fight left in me, but I have to try. "You can't have her," I insist, my voice barely a whisper. "You can't take Bailey."

Amos chuckles, and the sound makes my stomach turn. "I'm taking Bailey," it assures me. "And then you're both going to die."

Before I can react, the thing raises its free hand and presses its cold, slimy palm against my forehead.

A bolt of lightning splits the sky, and by the time the thunder rolls, I'm overtaken completely.

# 25

# THIS IS WHERE IT LIVES

Bailey

I NEED to get Tanner away from that house.

Bitter certainty floods my veins as I walk toward my car. Every nerve in my body screams at me that I'm making the wrong choice. But I can't just leave him there, not after what Layla's told me. I can't.

Making up my mind, I slide into the driver's seat. Adrenaline surges through me as I turn the key in the ignition, urging the engine to life. I try not to think too much about where I'm going and why. Instead, I focus on the muscle memory of backing out of the driveway and navigating the familiar streets of Hahnville.

Night's grip has tightened on the evening by the time I reach the turnoff to the old Gregory place. As I steer carefully down the rutted drive, my headlights play off the gnarled trunks of the cypress trees and the twisted mass of foliage at their roots. It feels like there are a thousand pairs of eyes on me, watching my descent into this unholy place.

My hands tighten on the wheel. I keep my gaze focused straight ahead at the muddy, potholed road. Whatever is out here tonight, I don't want to see it.

It's almost a relief when I come around the bend and finally catch sight of the house. It's my first time seeing it up close, and I have to admit that Tanner's descriptions of the structure haven't done it any justice.

The building is a masterpiece of stone, wood, and glass. While it's certainly not my style, I can still appreciate the craftsmanship that's gone into the construction. It looks like something out of a magazine, bone white and picture-perfect.

Tanner's comments about the house float to the forefront of my mind. He said something about how it looks great now, but in a few years, the swamp will overtake this place too.

I can imagine it. Soon there will be moss and ivy creeping up those sterile white walls. Mold and debris will overtake the perfect roof. Humidity will cloud the windows, and the stench of the swamp will infect the air. The ground, always soft from the constant moisture, will give out, and the foundation will crumble, and the house will sag and droop until it finally falls into the mire, just like everything else that has ever tried to live here.

This is not a place that was meant for people.

It never was.

For a moment, as I stare up at the imposing new house, I see it as it will be ten years down the line, rotting from the inside out. Then I blink, and the image is gone, and the building is gleaming and new again.

A shiver passes through me as my eyes are drawn down toward the front of the house. My heartbeat stutters as I recognize the truck that's parked outside the front door.

It's Tanner's.

He's here somewhere, but where? His vehicle appears empty. Beyond, the windows of the house are dark and vacant. There's no movement, no sign of life.

"Tanner is alive," I assure myself in a fervent whisper. "He's here. He has to be here."

I park my car behind Tanner's truck. I cut the engine and then hesitate for a moment before I decide to leave the keys in the ignition in case we need to make a quick getaway. With no signal out here at the moment, I decide to leave my phone in the car too. It's not like I can call for help even if I need to.

After a few anxious seconds, I gather my courage and push the car door open, breaking the last barrier between the swamp and me.

The first thing I notice as I step out onto the driveway is the silence. Normally, the night is alive with the drone of insects and the bustle of small nocturnal animals through the undergrowth. But tonight, there's no noise. It's like the entire world is holding its breath, waiting.

Or hiding.

The putrid smell of the swamp thickens as the heavy summer air swirls around me. Sweat beads on my forehead and my back. Each breath I take feels fuzzy and hot, like I'm taking in water with every lungful.

My footsteps crunch loudly as I pick my way over to Tanner's truck. As I guessed, the vehicle is unoccupied. Everything inside looks normal, undisturbed. I don't know if that's a good sign or a bad one.

Finding nothing there, I continue on to the front door of the house. It's closed, and I'm suddenly concerned that it might be locked. Do construction crews usually secure their job sites? I'm not entirely sure, but I assume they would, especially when the place is almost completely done.

I'm not sure if I'm relieved or worried to find that the door is unlocked. The metal doorknob, eerily warm from the stale night air, turns easily beneath my palm, and the door swings open smoothly without so much as a creak.

Darkness stretches before me, opening up into the vast unknown space of the rest of the house. The fine hairs on the back of my neck stand up as I sense eyes boring into me. I'm not alone here.

"Hello?" I call? My voice quivers away into the shadows until it's swallowed up completely. "Tanner?"

There's no answer.

I take a single step inside the door. With one hand, I grope around on the wall until my fingers trace over a light switch.

"Thank God," I breathe, flipping it on.

Nothing happens.

I try the switch again and then a third time, the clicks echoing hollowly into the dark. But still, the light doesn't turn on.

"Fuck," I mutter. I suddenly regret the decision to leave my phone in the car. I could really use the flashlight now. Maybe I should go get it?

But then a noise in the distance has me freeze on the threshold. Was it a sigh or a rustle of fabric? I'm not sure.

"Tanner?" I call again, taking another tentative step into the darkness.

I'm blind in here. The shadows swallow me up quickly, and I have to use a hand on the wall to navigate. I inch through the space slowly and carefully. The only respite I get is when I pass an open doorway and some moonlight from outside filters in through the windows. It feels like an eternity before I reach the back of the house and step into the kitchen.

Weak light tumbles in through the uncovered windows, illuminating a large space filled with gleaming new appliances and heavy marble countertops. But what really draws my attention is the figure standing a few feet away from the doorway.

"Tanner," I sigh in relief.

He's got his back to me so he's facing the wall. There's a large gap there in the sheetrock in the hallway right outside the kitchen, and I wonder if that's what he's stayed so late to fix. But if he was working, why was he here in the dark? Maybe a fuse blew?

Tanner doesn't move. There's no indication he's even heard me.

Fear curls across my nerves as I creep toward him, my hand outstretched. When I'm only about a foot away, I rest my fingertips gingerly on his shoulder.

"Tanner?" I murmur.

He turns slowly, and my dread only deepens when I catch sight of his face. His expression is slack and vacant at first but then snaps to life when he sees me. I have a terrible feeling that he's been like this for hours, just biding his time until I arrived.

"Bailey," he coos in a saccharine tone that sets my hair on end. "I'm so glad you're finally here. I've been waiting for you for a very long time."

He takes a step toward me, closing the distance between us. I stumble back.

"It's time to go, Tanner," I say, even though I have a sneaking suspicion that I'm no longer speaking to him.

"Go?" He cocks his head. "I don't think so, baby. In fact, I don't think we're ever going to leave."

Before I can act, his hands dart out and grab me to bring me in for a crushing kiss. I flail against him, trying to push off against his chest and arms, but his grip is like iron.

His mouth trails a bruising path to my ear where he growls, "Oh, Bailey, the things I'll do to you tonight. You'll never forget them, not even in death."

"Get off me!" I shriek, hammering against him. To my horror, I hear the sound of a zipper, and I instantly know what he's got in store for me.

I won't let that happen.

I jerk my knee up as hard and fast as I can directly between Tanner's legs.

A wail of pain erupts from his throat as he pushes me away from him. I don't stay to watch as he clutches at his groin, doubled over in agony. Instead, I dart out into the hallway toward the front door.

It doesn't take long for Tanner to right himself. He's like an animal as he surges behind me. I've got a head start, but he's faster than I am. Blood rushes in my ears as I push myself harder.

I'm almost to the front door.

I'm almost free.

But just as I reach the threshold, Tanner's fingers tangle in my hair. For a moment, I think he's going to pull me back, but instead, he jerks me forward.

My forehead smacks into the doorframe with a sickening thump. My skull erupts in pain, and I cry out sharply. Hot blood trickles down my skin. The world swims in front of my eyes, and then I'm drowning in the darkness.

Things undulate in and out of focus. One moment, Tanner's dragging me down the hallway by one arm, wrenching my shoulder in its socket. The next thing I know, I feel like I'm weightless.

I blink heavily, forcing my eyes open. My head throbs with pain. I'm upright, I think, my back leaning against a rough, unfinished wall. Where am I? Where has he taken me?

Tanner's face looms into view.

But it's not Tanner, not anymore.

"Amos," I choke out.

The thing controlling Tanner's body grins. "The one and only," it agrees. "Dalton's form was getting a little tired, wasn't it? I wanted something a little... fresher."

It leans down out of view, and when it straightens up, I realize with growing horror that it's holding a section of drywall.

I whip my head around, wincing at the sudden movement as I desperately take in my surroundings. I'm looking at the hallway by the kitchen, but I'm not at the right angle. I think about where Tanner was earlier, and the hole in the wall.

The pieces click together.

I'm not in the hallway at all.

I'm *inside* the wall.

And Amos is going to seal me in.

# 26

# WHAT I HAVE TO DO

Tanner

EVERYTHING IS FRAGMENTED, like I'm skipping through a movie and picking frames at random.

I'm not in the swamp anymore. Instead, I'm standing at the back of the house where the fuse boxes are.

How did I get here? The last thing I remember is Amos' hand against my forehead, pushing, *forcing*. My eyes trail out toward the cemetery, but there's no movement out there, no telltale shadows amidst the cypress trees.

Why am I here? At this point, I notice a weight in my hand and look down. To my confusion, I realize that I'm holding a hammer, gripping the handle so tightly that my knuckles have gone white.

I turn back to the fuse box, which is hanging open on one mangled hinge. The whole thing is destroyed. Bits of metal and plastic litter the dead grass underneath. A tang of burning electronics lingers in the air.

Did I do this? I have a vague impression of swinging the hammer, but no memory of an impact.

"What the fuck?" I groan as the tools slips from my grasp. My throat feels raw, as though I've been screaming, but I don't remember that either.

I blink, and when I open my eyes, I'm no longer in the backyard.

I'm in the driveway, nestled in the shadow of the house. Dusk curls across the horizon. Several hours must have passed since my brief moment of clarity by the fuse box, but I have no memory of how I spent them. All I know is that night will fall soon, and I don't want to be here when it does.

It's a good thing I'm in the driveway. I'll jump in my truck and get the hell out of this fucking place. Bailey will be waiting for me to pick her up at her mother's house, and then we'll finally be free and clear of Amos.

But when I turn toward my vehicle, my hopes plummet.

The hood of the truck is up. I'm certain I didn't leave it that way earlier. Dread builds inside of me, brick by heavy brick, as I approach the vehicle. One look under the hood only confirms my fears that most of the engine has been tampered with.

"Fuck!" I growl, kicking the side of the truck.

I think I know what Amos is trying to do. First the power, then my one means of escape. He's trying to keep me here, isolate me.

The hood clangs loudly as I let it down. If I can't take the truck out of here, I guess I'll have to walk. This afternoon's rain has softened the driveway to mud, but I'm already covered with slimy filth dredged up from the bottom of the swamp. It's not like I can get any grosser.

But before I can even make it a few steps, I blink, and the scene has once again shifted.

It's fully dark now. I'm standing in the kitchen of the house, staring into the hole in the wall. Dimly, I struggle to recall why I haven't finished putting up the new sheetrock yet, but I can't get my mind to focus. It's like somebody is inside my brain, trying to steer my thoughts in a different direction.

"Hello?" a voice calls from the front of the house. "Tanner?"

My blood chills. That's Bailey's voice. What the hell is she doing here?

"She's here for you," Amos's voice hisses in my ear. It's like he's in my brain and all around me, engulfing me in his putrescence. "She's here for us."

"No," I force out, so quietly that it's barely audible in the suffocating darkness of the kitchen.

Amos's grating laugh lances through my mind. I want to wince, but I can't move my face. In fact, I can't move at all.

"I want you to see this," the thing croons. "I want you to feel this."

Bailey's quivering voice rings through the house as she once again calls, "Tanner?"

I want to call out to her, to yell at her to run as fast and as far as she can. She's not safe here. Amos is in control, and I'm not sure I'll be able to stop him. I don't want him to hurt her.

*I* don't want to hurt her.

Careful footsteps echo down the hallway as Bailey creeps closer. I start to ask myself why she hasn't turned on any of the lights when I remember the busted fuse box out in the backyard. Amos did that using my body, I realize. Bile rises in my throat as I think about the destroyed engine of my truck.

Those things weren't meant for me. They were for Bailey. Amos wants her here, wandering around blindly in the dark with no way to leave. This is a game for him, a hunt.

And Bailey is his prey.

I hear her step across the threshold of the kitchen. "Tanner," she says in a relieved rush of breath when she catches sight of me. I want to turn around and tell her to get away from me, but I'm stuck here with my eyes locked on the hole in the wall.

"Tanner?" she repeats, her hand coming to rest tentatively on my shoulder.

My body turns toward her, but I'm not controlling the movements. I can feel hideous delight welling up inside of me, and I realize sickly that the anticipation belongs to Amos. Whatever he's planning for Bailey, he's going to enjoy every second of it.

"Bailey." The voice that comes out of my mouth sounds like mine, but the words belong to Amos. "I'm so glad you're finally here. I've been waiting for you for a very long time."

Using my body, Amos takes an imposing step toward Bailey. She's pale in the moonlight, her eyes wide with fear. Desperation and terror line her features, and I wonder if she knows this isn't really me, that Amos is pulling the strings.

"It's time to go, Tanner." She speaks slowly and carefully, as though she's addressing a wild animal.

I barely register whatever Amos says next. I know what he wants to do to her, and I'm determined to fight him every step of the way. Blood rushes in my ears as I struggle against the demon's hold over me. I almost don't notice that I've been talking and moving until Bailey's knee smashes into my crotch, sending stars dancing across my vision as pain bursts between my legs.

I double over, and for the briefest moment, my actions are my own.

*It's the pain! The demon can't use me when I'm in physical pain!*

The thought flickers quickly through my brain, planting the tiny seed of a plan. But then Amos is back in control, and I can only cry out in my own mind as he uses my body to chase Bailey down and smack her head into the doorframe.

Amos drags her by the arm into the kitchen before lifting her easily and dumping her semi-conscious body into the hole in the wall.

Was this his plan all along? Every time I'd try to fix the drywall, there would always be some problem, some reason I couldn't finish.

And now, as Bailey begs for her life, I realize that Amos truly has been waiting for a very long time.

I'm not going to let him get what he wants.

Amos is slowly but surely securing the fresh sections of sheetrock to cover the hole. He's already got the bottom panel finished and is now working on the middle. He's using the nail gun, the one that Terry had been working with earlier today.

Sour fear curls through my body as I realize what I have to do.

Amos is distracted, gloating to Bailey. She's terrified and confused. The sight of her with blood running down her face from the nasty gash in her scalp gives me the courage for what I do next.

I line the nail gun up with the back of my hand, but it's Amos who presses the trigger.

I let out a yowl of pain as the nail passes through my flesh. Almost immediately, I yank the metal out of my hand and let it fall to the ground with a clatter.

Bailey screams from inside the hole in the wall, but I can't understand what she's saying. It's taking every ounce of my focus to push Amos back.

Blinded by agony, I stumble out of the kitchen and into the hallway. I've worked on this project for so long that I know the layout of this house like the back of my hand. Killing the lights won't slow me down.

"You can't have her!" I howl as I scramble out the backdoor. "I'll die before you take her!"

And it's the truth. I can't hold Amos off forever. Even as my hand throbs where the nail pierced it, I can feel the demon clawing at my mind, trying desperately to get back in.

I can't let that happen. If I'm gone, Bailey will be safe. She'll hate me for what I've done, for what Amos has made me do, but she'll survive. That's the only thing that's important right now.

Bailey.

The dead grass is slick beneath my boots as I claw my way across the backyard. At long last, I feel the suck of mud at my feet and the welcome rush of water that tells me I've reached the swamp. Despite Amos tearing at my mind, I push forward, wading through the water until I pull myself up onto the mossy outcropping of the cemetery.

If I go any farther out into the marsh, the water will be deeper and more treacherous. It's my only option.

"Don't do it!" Amos snarls.

I laugh into the night. It's a demented noise, the sound of man driven to madness. "Or what?" I shout into the night. "You'll kill me? You'll kill Bailey?"

"I can give you anything you desire," he wheedles. He's desperate now, his emotions leeching back into mine. He knows what I'm planning, but the pain in my hand is too great for him to take me back fully.

"Anything?" I ask. I'm panting with exertion as I haul myself up using one of the crumbling tombstones for leverage. I'm worried the mossy stone will give beneath my weight, but it holds.

"Anything," Amos promises.

I turn my back to the cemetery and the house beyond. When I squint out into the darkness, all I can see is black water and the trunks of the cypress trees rising from the swamp like the rib bones of some huge, ancient creature.

Let the roots be my pallbearers and the mud be my mausoleum.

"I'll tell you what I want," I shout into the night.

"Anything, anything," Amos assures me.

I stare down into the depths of the mire. "I want you to go to hell."

And then I jump, losing myself to the embrace of the swamp.

27

———————

# KILLING IT

Bailey


THERE'S SO MUCH BLOOD.

Oh God, there's so much blood.

I'm screaming, and I can't seem to stop. My head swims at the sight of the nail gouged into Tanner's hand. His agonized howls pierce through my skull in jagged bolts as he flails and fights against something I can't see.

And then he's gone, staggering out into the night with only incoherent shouts trailing in his wake.

I need to move. I need to get out of this fucking place.

Groaning, I struggle to my feet and assess the situation. Amos, using Tanner's body, managed to fix a panel of drywall to the bottom of the small space, and it's too high for me to simply step over.

I gather my strength and then kick out at the sheetrock. It splits with a sharp crack. At the same time, I cry out as pain shoots through my ankle and zings up my shin.

"Fuck!" I sob, bracing myself in the small space as my foot begins to throb.

But I don't stop.

I *can't* stop.

Somehow, Tanner must have broken Amos's hold over him. I don't know how he did it, but when I stared up at Tanner just before he put the nail through his hand, I was absolutely sure that it was the man I love looking back at me.

But how long can he hold Amos off for?

A shudder runs through me as I imagine the demon sinking his claws into Tanner again. And if he does, will he turn around and come after me? Would he try to destroy Tanner for defying him?

I can't let either of those things happen.

Grimacing in pain, I drag myself out of the hole in the wall, through the hallway, and into the moonlit kitchen.

It isn't hard to figure out where Tanner has gone. Blood has dribbled down from his wounded hand and left a blotchy trail for me to follow. The spots are almost black in the moonlight, starkly visible against the white tile of the floor.

I stagger through the house step by tortuous step. My ankle protests, and I think I can feel the bones grinding as I move, but I grit my teeth and force myself forward in spite of the pain.

The blood leads me through the backdoor and into the yard. I nearly slip on the damp dead grass but right myself before I can fall. I pause there, squinting out into the night.

Where is he?

A sloshing noise reaches my ears, the sound of somebody wading through the muck of the swamp. I turn toward the disturbance and am just able to make out the familiar shape of Tanner as he stumbles through the mud and waist-high water.

My heart sinks as I realize that he's heading toward the cemetery. The crumbling tombstones beckon him, rising up from the hazy, humid darkness like the jagged teeth of a slumbering beast.

If he makes it to that island, the demon will consume him.

Ignoring the pain in my ankle, I fling myself into the swamp. I don't know what I'll do when I reach Tanner, but I know I have to try to stop him.

Water closes around my legs. Mud reaches up to pull at my feet as I wade deeper, coaxing me to stay. I feel like I'm in the stomach of something unfathomable, being slowly digested the further I go. And it's true, in a way. Even if we make it out of this hellish place, the swamp has already taken me. I'll never be whole again.

But it can't have all of me.

I grab onto one of the gravestones and pull myself up onto the mossy clearing just as Tanner jumps into the deeper marsh beyond.

"No!" I scream, reaching for him.

But my fingers grasp empty air as the water rushes over him.

He floats there for a moment, his face bone-white beneath the surface. Then he jerks as though he's been punched in the stomach. Mud churns around him and bubbles froth from his mouth as he struggles, blurring the scene.

"Tanner!" I throw myself down on my belly and plunge my arms into the water, feeling blindly for him, but I can't figure out where he's gone.

I pull back to watch and catch a glimpse of him a few feet away beneath the surface.

But he's not alone.

He's grappling with a shadowy figure, one I've seen in my dreams.

Amos, wearing a poorly rendered version of Dalton's body, has his arms locked around Tanner. I can't tell if he's trying to hold Tanner down or drag him to the surface.

As if he senses my presence, Amos turns his ghoulish face up to mine and grins. In a flash, he pushes Tanner deeper into the brackish sludge and surges upward.

I barely have time to blink before he's on me.

His hands, cold and slick, close around my throat. I flail against him, shredding the skin of his wrists beneath my nails, but instead of drawing blood, the greenish ooze of the swamp leaks out of his veins.

"Finally," Amos crows, his face hovering only inches from mine. His breath is the stench of the marsh, of dead things returning to the soil.

I can't fight this. I have no weapons, and the only person who could possibly help is somewhere under the water.

I'm powerless.

Amos's fingers tighten around my throat, cutting off my air completely. Black spots erupt before my eyes. The throbbing in my head intensifies.

*Help me. Please, anybody! Help me!*

The silent plea plays through my mind again and again as my body begins to slacken in the demon's grasp.

I'm going to die here.

My eyes flutter closed as I finally accept the crushing reality. Will anybody notice I'm gone? Will anybody come looking for me?

Helen will, I think. I'd promised to call her once we made it to Layla's. She'll know something's wrong.

*Wait.*

Helen.

Helen had told me something important, hadn't she?

My oxygen-starved brain struggles to dredge up the memory of us sitting in the kitchen, a piece of paper in front of us.

Words, strange words. A spell.

*A weapon.*

I can't speak, but I picture the paper in my head. My mouth moves soundlessly as I trace the curves and sharp edges of the letters, willing them to be heard by something, anything.

My nerves, dulled by the lack of air, erupt with sudden electricity. Energy whips through me, crackling over my skin and churning my blood as I chant silently into the night.

"What...?" Amos gasps. His hands loosen around my neck.

Greedily sucking in the heavy night air, I take the opportunity to speak the incantation aloud. The syllables slide out in a coarse whisper, echoing across the water in terse ripples.

*"From light to shadow, from stone to bone,*

*I send you back to the void you've known.*

*By earth, by sky, by sea, I proclaim,*

*Be gone, demon, in darkness remain."*

"No." Amos is staring at me, his face lined with incredulous hatred. "No!"

Power builds inside of me. I feel incandescent as the words flow out of my mouth and into the darkness. The branches of the cypress trees shiver. Insects buzz in a feverish frenzy as the creatures that call the swamp home cry out in a hellish cacophony of sound.

In that moment, I realize that what Helen had said about this place is true. The swamp is ancient, unfathomable. Amos, Asmodeus, whatever it calls itself, might be old, but the power I tap into now is eternal.

Not even a demon can withstand the call of time.

"No!" Amos howls as his body is drawn backward. To my horror, I see that cypress roots have tangled around his legs and are pulling him back toward the dark water. Mud trickles upward in veiny rivulets, creeping across its pale skin in brackish tracks.

There are a million things I want to say in that moment, but I just keep chanting, my voice wailing above the roar of the marsh. The power gathers to a peak, and I feel myself teetering on the edge of something huge and beyond my understanding.

*"From light to shadow, from stone to bone,*

*I send you back to the void you've known.*

*By earth, by sky, by sea, I proclaim,*

*Be gone, demon, in darkness remain."*

"Fuck you!" I scream, unleashing the tidal wave of energy in one terrible, devastating tsunami.

Wind whips through the cemetery. Amos lets out an inhuman screech as the roots and the mud suck his form down into the water. I watch as his wild, pale face disappears into impossible depths, something beneath the swamp itself.

And then it's over.

The trees shudder into stillness. The insects and animals are silent once again. The muddy water ripples out to a smooth, matte plane.

*Tanner!*

His absence strikes me hard as I realize that he hasn't surfaced. How long has it been? Seconds? Minutes?

"Tanner!" I call desperately, scanning the water for him. "Tanner?"

There's no sign of him. Fear wells inside of me as I imagine him on the bottom of the swamp, gone forever.

I don't stop to think about what to do next. I simply throw my aching, spent body forward into the water, toward the man I love.

Brackish liquid seeps into my mouth and nose. I force my eyes open against the grit. There's barely any visibility down here, so I reach out and grope blindly through the mud. My fingers catch roots and rocks and things I can't even identify, and then finally I brush the fabric of Tanner's shirt.

Without hesitating, I grab his arm and kick up off the slimy bottom, propelling us upward.

We breach the surface in a surge of mud and water. Spluttering, I heave him toward the cemetery, using one of the gravestones to leverage him onto the mossy ground.

"Tanner?" I drop to my knees beside him, my hands coming up to frame his face.

He's still, so still.

I feel for his pulse and find nothing.

"No," I sob. "Tanner, no, you can't. Don't leave me, please!"

I want to break down, but there's no time for that. I'm a nurse. I've treated drowning victims before. I know I need to act fast if there's any hope of bringing him back.

Steeling myself, I pinch his nose shut and lean down to breathe life into his lungs. Then I pump his chest like I've done so many times before, chanting the beats out into the night.

"One, two, three, four, five."

Another breath, another set of palpitations.

"One, two, three, four, five."

I think of the power that had surged through me earlier. Was there any of that left? Would it answer if I called again?

"One, two, three, four, five."

*Please.*

*Please!*

"One, two, three, four, five."

On the final pump, Tanner's body spasms as muddy water erupts from his mouth.

He retches again, and I roll him on his side so he doesn't choke. Tears of relief flow down my face as his eyes flutter open.

"Tanner?" I ask, gently cupping his face in my hands. "Baby? Can you hear me?"

"Yeah," he coughs weakly.

It's the best sound I've heard all day.

## 28

# THE AFTERMATH

Tanner

MY EYELIDS CLOSE for what I'm sure is the last time as the swamp swallows me whole.

I blink, and I wake up from the nightmare of mud and mire to see an angel.

Bailey is smiling down at me, her eyes shining with relief and love. Muck from the swamp covers every inch of her, and brackish water drips from her hair.

She's the most beautiful creature I've ever seen.

"Tanner?" she asks, her voice hushed and quiet as though she's by a patient's bedside. "Baby? Can you hear me?"

"Yeah," I sputter. My lungs are on fire, and my mouth tastes like I've been licking a sewage pipe. What the fuck happened? The last thing I remember is Amos trying to take me over again.

*Amos.*

Fear rushes through me, and I grip Bailey's hands desperately.

"Where's Amos?" I wheeze as my eyes dart around, trying to catch a glimpse of the demon in the shadows.

"Gone," she replies firmly, her face grim. "I kicked his fucking ass."

"Good," I sigh, settling back against the mossy soil. My whole body aches. All I want to do is sleep.

"But I'm not sure if he's dead," Bailey continues, nudging me to sit up. "And I don't want to stay to find out."

As tempting as it is to rest for a little while longer, I can't help but share her concern. "How did you do it?"

A haunted look passes across Bailey's face. For a split second, I have the distinct feeling that she's somehow so far away, she has one foot in another world entirely. But then she shakes her head, and the uncanny expression slides from her features.

"I'm not sure," she shrugs, though I'm not convinced. "It was some spell that Helen gave me. It was... weird."

"Spell?" I repeat. I think back to all of those nights alone in our bed while Bailey watched over Robert Wilson. It made sense that Helen had known about the demon here. She's lived on the edge of the swamp for quite a while. Of course, she's seen things, knows things.

Bailey nods. "But like I said before, I'm not sure if this is permanent." She glances back over her shoulder toward the dark, still water of the marsh. "We really should get out of here."

After what's happened to us tonight, I have to agree.

Sitting up is a strenuous task. My whole body aches, and my head pounds. The heavy, stagnant taste in my mouth is so bad that I have to suppress the urge to gag even as bile rises in the back of my throat.

But the worst pain radiates from the palm of my left hand. There's a thin, ragged hole running clean through my flesh. Blood pulses out in time with my uneven heartbeat, mixing with the putrid mud that clings to my skin.

"Oh my god, Tanner," Bailey gasps as she catches sight of the wound.

"I'm fine," I say, though we both know that's a lie.

"I'll patch it up once we get to the car," she promises. "If we leave it like that for too long, it'll probably get infected."

I nod in agreement. I don't even want to think about the things floating down there in the stinking water.

Bailey helps me stagger to my feet. My legs are unsteady and weak beneath me, and my head swims dangerously as I try to find my balance. Finally, I'm able to stumble forward a few steps. As long as Bailey keeps her arm around me, I think we'll be able to make it to the car.

Navigating the swamp turns out to be trickier than I'd imagined. It takes almost ten minutes for the two of us to slog through the marshy landscape. By the time we reach the dead brown grass of the backyard, I'm ready to fall to my knees and kiss the solid earth beneath our feet.

But Bailey doesn't stop to let me rest. Instead, she hauls me across the lawn and around the side of the house.

"My truck!" I remember frantically, drawing to an unsteady halt. "Amos fucked with my truck!" My heart sinks as I realize we'll have to hobble down the long, rutted driveway together in order to get out of this hellish place.

"Leave it," Bailey says, shaking her head. "We'll take my car."

Her car?

Sure enough, as we round the side of the house and step onto the gravel of the driveway, I catch sight of her sedan gleaming in the low moonlight. Of course, she drove here to find me. I'm obviously not thinking clearly still. Hopefully, Amos didn't make me tamper with that vehicle too.

Bailey leads me around to the passenger side. Part of me is terrified that Amos isn't really gone, that he's just toying with us and that the door won't open when Bailey goes to pull the handle, but it swings open easily. A relieved sigh rushes from my aching lungs as I lower myself into the seat.

After closing the door behind me, Bailey runs around the front of the car and slides into the passenger seat. As she turns the key in the ignition, the interior lights come on momentarily, and I gasp in horror as I realize the state she's in.

There's a thick gash on her forehead. Her blood mingles with the mud of the swamp and clots in her hair. The bandage around her wrist and hand has loosened. I catch a glimpse of the swollen, bruised skin beneath and wince. I wonder if there are other wounds that I can't see, ones that run even deeper.

"I did this to you," I murmur, shame welling in my chest. I reach out my good hand toward the cut on her forehead, my fingers hovering only centimeters above the split skin.

Bailey closes her eyes and shakes her head. "No," she whispers fervently. "It wasn't you. It was Amos."

I know there's truth to what she's saying. No matter how much time might pass, I don't think I'll ever be able to forget the demon's claws sinking into my brain, gouging at the deepest parts of myself until I had become something unrecognizable, something inhuman. That horrible, grating laugh will forever haunt me.

No matter how far we run, I know deep down that I've left a part of myself out there in that festering swamp, and I'll never be whole again.

There was nothing down there but death.

I shudder as I recall how the slimy water closed in above my head, stealing the last vestiges of moonlight as I sank deeper into the abyss. It was peaceful, in a way. The cold certainty of my decision was almost comforting. Even if I couldn't remember them all, even if I hadn't been in control, I knew that I'd done some terrible things. Would sacrificing myself for the woman I love be the worst way to atone for my sins?

As the oxygen in my lungs started to run its course, my mind began to wander. How long would it take for me to drown? I had no idea, but I guessed I was about to find out.

But then, as I neared the murky bottom of the swamp, the water rushed around me as something solid came in contact with my stomach.

Bubbles rushed from my lips toward the surface as gritty, foul-tasting liquid flooded my mouth. My lungs burned as the water hit them. I wanted to cough, but I couldn't. There was no air. Oh God, *there was no air.*

Hands closed around my shoulders, and I flailed wildly. My foot hit the bottom of the marsh, kicking up clouds of sediment around us. But I didn't need to see to know that it was Amos.

The demon buffeted me back and forth. Mud and water frothed around us. I didn't know which way was up or down. My heart pounded, and my lungs felt like they were about to explode from my chest.

And then it stopped.

I didn't know where Amos went. I couldn't bring myself to care.

Darkness crept across the edges of my vision. I tried to reach out, to feel for the sludgy bottom of the swamp, but my limbs were heavy and nonresponsive.

There was nothing down there but death....

I snap from the memory with almost painful clarity.

"I'm sorry," I choke out. "I'm so fucking sorry, Bailey."

I'm sorry for hurting her. I'm sorry for accepting this fucking job in the first place, for getting us into this mess. I'm sorry for not being strong enough to fight Amos properly, for insisting on taking one more day, for being so blind.

Bailey's eyes flash in the moonlight. "You have nothing to apologize for," she tells me firmly, catching my hand in her own. She laces her fingers between mine. "It was Amos. All of this was Amos."

How can she just wave it all away like that? The sickening crack of her forehead meeting the doorframe earlier tonight rings through my head. I don't deserve her forgiveness. I don't deserve her love.

I squeeze my eyes closed and recall the surety I'd felt earlier when I'd tumbled off the mossy bank of the cemetery and into the water. I would've died for her.

Maybe now I have a chance to live for her, too.

"I love you," I whisper. My voice disperses into the darkness, teetering somewhere between a plea and a prayer.

Bailey smiles softly. "I love you too," she murmurs, squeezing my hand tighter in her grasp.

My body relaxes into the passenger seat as I let out a relieved sigh. But we're not out of the woods yet. "What do we do now?" I ask.

"We get the hell out of here," she replies quickly. Her gaze creeps to the edge of the swamp in the distance, as though she expects to see Amos standing there amidst the shadowy tombstones, ready to fuck with us some more.

"I couldn't agree more," I mutter, scowling out at the tangled snarl of cypress trees. Once we make it down the driveway, I know we're never coming back to this place.

I can't help thinking back to the first time I ever stepped foot here. It had been the night of the fire. I'd done everything in my power to save the structure and stop the spread of the flames.

Letting it all burn didn't even make a difference.

Bailey, unaware of my wandering mind, turns to me. "I think we should go to Layla's," she suggests. "Florida. We can stay with her and Dalton for a bit, just until we can find a place of our own. What do you say?"

I watch her as she considers me carefully, waiting for my response. In that moment, Bailey is more beautiful than I've ever seen her. Her eyes flash with defiant strength, and my blood surges as I realize how sexy empowerment looks on her. She could've told me we'd be going to the goddamn moon, and I'd agree.

"I'll follow you anywhere," I breathe before closing the distance to capture her lips in a passionate kiss.

# 29

# THE STATE OF SUNSHINE

Bailey

"TANNER!" I yell, hoping he can hear me in the next room.

I'm frozen in fear, unable to move as I stare up at my enemy.

"Tanner!" I scream again.

Summoned by my shouts of terror, Tanner bursts into the room. His muscular body is tense, his arms raised and ready to fight. But then he catches sight of my mortal foe and relaxes into a relieved grin.

"Seriously, babe?" he asks in a teasing tone, shaking his head. "A spider?"

I glare at him, finally taking my eyes off the eight-legged freak that's been making itself at home on the ceiling of our brand new living room. "What?" I snap as he struggles not to laugh at my predicament.

"Bailey, you fought a literal demon. And now you're afraid of a little bug?" he chuckles.

"It's not little," I huff, but his mood is contagious, and I can't help but crack a smile. He's right. It is pretty ridiculous. Nevertheless, he scoops the arachnid up in a cup and carries it carefully outside, releasing it in the driveway as I watch from the safety of the hallway.

"Better?" he asks as he slips back through the front door.

"Much," I confirm, sealing it with a kiss.

He follows me to the living room where I've been unpacking a box of books. My mom was kind enough to bundle up all our worldly possessions and ship them over to Florida as soon as we'd found a place.

It's hard to believe that we've made it this far. It's only been a few months since we fled from the old Gregory place in my car, leaving Hahnville far behind us. We drove for hours, not daring to stop until we pulled up outside of Layla's. She and Dalton let us stay for a while, and we took the time to search for a place to call our own.

And now we have it.

I beam at Tanner, who smiles warmly in return. His eyes, once cold and distant under Amos's influence, sparkle with life. He had no problem moving his company to our new state. He's already gotten licensed, picked up a ton of new jobs, and even has one coming up where he'll be working with Dalton to restore a crumbling old mansion to its former glory.

Tanner hasn't been the only one finding work these days. Layla put a good word in for me with the care center she contracts for, and they took me on right away. I love the job and have even made a few new friends since the move.

"Are you finished in the kitchen?" I ask Tanner as I stack some more books onto one of the empty shelves by the television.

"Yep," he nods, settling on the arm of the couch. "Everything we need for tonight is ready to go."

I chew on my lip, suddenly anxious. "Even the silverware?"

"Even the silverware," he assures me easily. He swoops down from his perch to capture my mouth with his. "Just relax, Bailey. Tonight is going to go great. And even if it doesn't, we'll look back on it later on and laugh."

His words have me melting into his arms as love wells in my chest. Still, I mumble, "I just want everything to be perfect."

I stare down at the shiny new ring adorning the ring finger of my left hand. Tanner got down on one knee yesterday as soon as the movers left. Overcome with happiness, I was barely able to speak, but I showed him my resounding yes in other, more physical ways. And now tonight, we're having Layla and Dalton over for dinner to give them the great news.

Tanner kisses me again, longer and more passionately than before. When he breaks away, I'm panting. "Everything is already perfect," he murmurs as he nuzzles the soft curve of my neck. "You're perfect."

A soft moan tumbles from my lips. This man has me coming undone with just his voice alone. As though he can feel the effect he has on me, Tanner chuckles against my skin and traces a burning trail of kisses over the arc of my collarbone.

I watch Tanner's southerly progression through my lashes. I'm going to marry this man. The realization hits me hard in the best possible way. We haven't talked about a date or anything yet, but soon, he'll be my husband, and I'll be his wife. I can picture us growing old here in this cute little house. Imaginary children swirl through my mind, promises of what's to come. Every vision just cements my surety.

"I love you," I breathe as Tanner's hands gently ease the straps of my sundress off my shoulders.

"And I love you," he replies, accentuating his words with another searing kiss. Meanwhile, his hands are busy unzipping the back of my dress.

The thin fabric falls away, and I'm suddenly glad that I chose not to wear a bra today. Tanner drinks in the sight of my exposed flesh like a man thirsting in the desert before he dives in for a taste.

"Tanner!" My hands weave into his hair as his mouth closes over one of the tender peaks of my breasts. I writhe beneath him, wanting more. Ever obliging, Tanner's rough palm courses up my thigh and between my legs. He strokes one finger against the damp cloth of my panties, and I shudder at his teasing touch.

Frustrated, my hands roam down his muscular shoulders to the buttons of his shirt. I'm barely able to focus on the task at hand, not with his tongue swirling around me like that. Finally, I manage to get his shirt open, revealing the firm planes of his chest.

Tanner growls at my touch, and the sound ignites my blood to boiling. Emboldened, I let my fingers wander lower, following the coarse hair trailing down his stomach until I find the zipper of his jeans. Without breaking away from his ministrations, I part the stiff fabric.

"Fuck," Tanner groans as his cock is freed from the confines of the denim. "Fuck!" he repeats as my fingers wrap around his girth and begin to move. His hips tip forward in time with the pumping of my hand as I tease him with the promise of what's to come.

After a few breathless moments, Tanner closes his fingers around my arm, stopping me. "Bed. Now," he pants.

He doesn't wait for me to agree. Instead, he scoops me up off the floor and carries me, bridal style, into the bedroom. I giggle as he tosses me onto the mattress.

"Now, where were we?" he grins as he lowers himself down on top of me. His legs nudge my knees apart, and he settles between my thighs. His cock strains against the thin fabric of my panties as his mouth claims mine with feverish abandon. I lift my hips to meet his and moan at the friction.

It's not enough.

"More," I beg, clutching at Tanner's broad shoulders.

"More?" he teases, his eyes sparkling with mischief. "Like this?"

His hand finds my center again. This time, he slides my panties to one side and dips a finger into my slick heat. I cry out in pleasure and then watch, my chest heaving, as he brings the finger to his lips and sucks it clean. It's the single sexiest thing I've ever seen.

"Or did you mean, like this?" he continues. His fingers hook around the edge of my panties. I lift my hips eagerly, allowing him to slide them off me completely. Before I can even consider what he might do next, his tongue darts out for a taste.

"Tanner!" I moan.

His mouth is too busy to reply. I squeeze my eyes shut against the onslaught of pleasure as his tongue works against my cunt. For a minute, the only noises in the room are the sinful mewls tumbling from my lips and the lascivious, wet sounds from between my legs.

Tension builds in my muscles as I feel my orgasm approaching. Tanner, sensing the change in my body, picks up the pace, drawing me closer and closer to the edge.

I shatter against his mouth as a wave of pleasure engulfs me.

He doesn't give me any time to recover. There's only a short pause as he kicks off his jeans completely, and then he's on top of me. The feel of his skin against mine quickly reignites the spark inside of me. My nerves sing as he positions himself against my entrance.

"Bailey," he breathes as he slides inside of me, inch by agonizing inch. The way he utters my name like a prayer has me clenching around him, and he groans wantonly into my ear. "You feel fucking amazing."

I crane my neck up and catch him in a kiss. It's slow and heady but quickly deepens as Tanner begins to thrust in earnest. Every stroke reawakens me, drawing me back toward the perilous edge.

My breath comes in short gasps as Tanner's cock hits just the right spot inside of me. His eyes are locked on mine, his gaze hot and unrelenting. Just when I think I can't possibly last any longer, he tilts his hips at the perfect angle, and I'm undone beneath him.

"Tanner!" I cry as my orgasm crashes over me.

"Fuck," he groans, speeding up as his rhythm becomes more erratic. A few seconds later, he growls, "Fuck, Bailey." He spills himself inside of me, and I moan again at the sensation.

Tanner's weight rests on top of me as he catches his breath. His presence is comforting and sure. We could stay here forever, wrapped in each other's arms until the end of time.

"I love you," I whisper, placing a gentle, almost chaste kiss on his brow.

Nuzzling his head into the crook of my neck, he replies, "I love you, Bailey. More than you'll ever know."

I want to linger there, ensconced in the feel of him, but Tanner reluctantly rolls onto his side and sits up.

"Where are you going?" I ask as I admire the unobstructed view of his broad shoulders.

"We can't lie in bed forever," Tanner shrugs. "We've only got fifteen minutes before Layla and Dalton get here."

"Shit!" I squeal. I'd been so caught up in the pleasure of the moment that I'd completely forgotten about our guests. "I haven't even started dinner yet!"

Tanner chuckles as I spring up. He wraps a strong arm around my waist and draws me back into his lap. His cock, still hard, presses tantalizingly against the curve of my ass. His tongue swipes at the shell of my ear, and I shiver.

"Then again," he murmurs wickedly. "There's a lot we could accomplish in fifteen minutes." He punctuates his words with a heavy thrust of his hips.

Fifteen minutes.

Something tells me we'll make the most of them. Layla and Dalton will just have to wait, southern hospitality be damned.

After all, what's fifteen minutes out of forever?

# 30

## JULIA AND JAKE

JULIA

I HATE THIS PLACE.

As the movers scurry about, hauling boxes and expensive furniture under Jake's watchful eye, I lounge in a deck chair with a glass of lemonade in one hand, trying not to cry.

This whole place is ghastly, no matter where I turn. The landscapers had been out a few weeks earlier and had turned the backyard where I'm currently sitting into a patchwork of sod. Unfortunately, it hadn't taken, and the grass is now dead and lifeless. Beyond, the yard gives way to mud and marsh. Cypress trees rise up in gnarled fingers, their roots hidden by murky sludge. Insects whine and drone amid the greenish haze.

I won't even let myself think about those dreadful tombstones. Jake's been arguing with the town for permission to remove the cemetery, but so far, he hasn't been able to cut through the red tape.

I take another sip of lemonade and then press the side of the sweating glass against my forehead. How is it so hot? It's early

November. Even the mountains of snow we had while staying in Upstate New York for most of the fall would be preferable to this moist, unrelenting heat.

Thinking wistfully of our large rental home back in New England and the pile of winter clothes that will be sitting, untouched, in my new closet for the foreseeable future, I find myself wishing that I'd added a splash of whiskey to the lemonade.

"Babe?" A voice calls, jerking me from my regrets. I turn in my chair to see Jake trundling down the lawn. He cuts a hell of a figure in that perfectly tailored suit and those sunglasses that cost more than what most people make in a week. How is it that I'm sitting out here, sweating my ass off, while he looks absolutely perfect? Life just isn't fair.

I paste on a fake smile, doing my best to dazzle him. "How's it going in there?" I ask, trying to sound genuinely curious.

Ignoring my question, Jake reaches for my glass. "Is that lemonade? Thanks!" Before I can protest, he downs the rest of the liquid and hands the empty glass back to me. "That hit the spot."

It takes all my willpower not to roll my eyes at him. "Is it coming together?" I press, nodding back toward the house.

"Don't worry your pretty little head about it," he assures me, as though I'm actually concerned. In all honesty, I'd have been delighted if he'd said that the movers had lost all of our earthly possessions, and we'd have to go back to New York after all. Moving back to Florida is no longer an option since he sold the home we had there.

"Do you think they'll finish today?" I question. I'm secretly hoping that the movers take their sweet time, forcing us to stay in a hotel for one last night.

Unfortunately for me, Jake nods enthusiastically. "Oh yeah," he says. "They've got most of the furniture set up. In fact, they're working on our bedroom right now." Even with his sunglasses hiding his eyes, I can feel his heated gaze raking over me.

I look up at him, and this time I can't keep the distaste off my face.

"I know Hahnville wasn't your first choice," he says earnestly. "But let's give it a shot. Six months. If you still hate it here, we can sell this place and find somewhere else to build our dream home. What do you say?"

"Six months?" I ask, crossing my arms.

He nods.

My eyes creep past him toward the swamp. It looks practically prehistoric out there, like some monstrous green dinosaur is going to come crashing through the underbrush at any moment. The headstones, tall thin antiques covered with centuries of moss and lichen, loom out of the misty, greenish shadows. I haven't even seen the marsh at night yet.

I don't think I want to.

"Fine," I utter, my eyes fluttering closed. "I'll give it six months, but not one second longer." Though my words sound resolute, trepidation stalks through my veins. Somehow, I feel like I've just made the biggest mistake of my life.

But I'm distracted as Jake's fingers curl under my chin. He tips my face up so that my lips brush his. His tongue swipes at the seam of my mouth, demanding entrance. I quickly oblige, more out of duty than for passion's sake at the moment.

When he breaks away, he grins saucily at me. "I'll let you know when the movers are done," he promises before sauntering back toward the house.

God, it won't be long enough.

I contemplate my situation as the afternoon wears on. Jake and I met in college. He was a business major gearing up to take over his father's finance company, and I'd studied English. His lavish gifts and passionate promises lured me into a whirlwind courtship and an early marriage. It strikes me now that I hadn't even had time to get to know the real Jake before we exchanged vows.

If I had, would I still have married him?

It pains me to admit that the answer was a solid maybe. I live quite comfortably, and that is certainly worth something. Over the years, I've become accustomed to the manicures, shopping sprees, and the relative freedom of not being chained to a desk from 9:00 to 5:00. In return, Jake shows me off to all of his important friends, and I do my best to please him in the bedroom, though it sometimes feels like a chore rather than a delight.

Sure, Jake can be kind of an asshole, but I'm used to him and his peculiarities. He's never been outright mean to me, never abusive or nasty. A lot of women have it much worse.

Guilt washes over me as I admonish myself for being so ungrateful, but a smaller voice still whispers that maybe I deserve to be happier. Maybe I deserve something more.

*Maybe, maybe, maybe.*

I'm so lost in my troubled thoughts that I nearly jump out of my skin as a hand closes around my shoulder.

"Whoa, babe. It's just me," Jake says, holding his palms out to me in a cartoonish gesture of disarmament.

"Sorry," I sigh, shaking my head. "I didn't hear you." My gaze shifts to the house. The windows stare blankly back. "Are the movers done?"

Jake nods. "All done," he confirms. "Come take a look."

Leaving the empty lemonade glass by the chair, I take his offered hand and allow him to lead me across the depressing, wilted lawn toward the open back door.

As we step inside, I have to admit that it looks great. Though the construction has taken absurdly long, it's all done masterfully. The furniture, which I've spent months picking out and changing my mind and swapping around, is exactly as I'd imagined.

Perhaps living here won't be so dreadful after all.

Jake doesn't stop to let me explore the cavernous rooms. Instead, he all but drags me to the stairs. I know exactly what he has in mind, so I follow him demurely as we climb up to the third floor.

"What do you think?" my husband asks as he steers me into the master bedroom.

"Oh, wow," I breathe.

It really does look lovely. Everything is done up in my favorite modern style. Colors range from deep black to slate grey and pristine white. The bed is huge and inviting. A small sitting area takes up the other half of the room. If I draw the thick drapes over the window to block the view of the swamp, maybe I can pretend that this really is our dream home.

As I wander around the space, Jake makes a beeline for the sitting area. I notice he's already prepped it with a bottle of expensive champagne in an ice bucket sitting alongside two crystal flutes. He pops the cork and pours each of us a glass. Before he brings me mine, he presses a few buttons on his phone and turns on the surround sound. The dulcet tones of Frank Sinatra fill the room as he hands me my glass.

"To new beginnings," he toasts, holding his flute up.

"New beginnings," I agree, tapping the edge of my glass against his. As I take a sip, Jake wraps his free arm around my waist, drawing me in closer and swaying me in time to the music. Not wanting to spill my champagne, I set the crystal flute down on the small table, and he does the same.

For the second time that day, Jake's lips find mine.

I try to find the sweetness in it, but it's a tall order. Jake is often selfish in bed, but it's never unpleasant. Still, I can't get my mind off where we are. I don't know if I'm in the mood to have sex when there's a cemetery right outside my window.

But as the Sinatra song ends and a haunting, bluesy melody flows through the speaker, Jake's kiss deepens into something more desperate. He seems lost in the lyrics as the rich voice begins to roll.

*Folks, I'm goin' down to St. James Infirmary, see my baby there...*

A small gasp of surprise escapes me as Jake's lips trail down my neck toward my collarbone. He nips at the sensitive skin there, and to my embarrassment, I can't suppress the moan that tumbles from my mouth.

Spurred by my noises, Jake begins pulling at the hem of my dress. He draws away for me only long enough to pull the expensive garment over my head and toss it away, and then he's back, his lithe form pressed against every inch of me.

This time, when his lips meet mine, I kiss him back with equal fervor. A part of me that's been slumbering for far too long stirs as Jake's hands ghost over my breasts, teasing my nipples through the thin, lacy fabric.

*She's stretched out on a long, white table...*

Jake backs me up until my knees hit the edge of the bed. Understanding his silent command, I fall back onto the mattress. When I look up at him, his eyes are clouded with lust. It's sexy as hell, and I'm surprised as a rush of heat blossoms at the juncture of my thighs.

Without breaking his gaze, Jake slides my panties down my legs. The graze of his nails against my sensitive skin is like sweet torture. I squirm in anticipation as his hands dance toward my center, and then cry out as he finally dips a finger inside.

"Jake," I moan, gripping at the sheets as he pumps his digit in and out of me. He doesn't usually do things like this, and it's driving me fucking wild. Pleasure builds as my nerves fray from the onslaught of sensation. Just when I'm inching toward the point of no return, Jake removes his hand.

I'm not expecting what comes next. In one swift, breathtaking motion, Jake flips me over onto my belly. Unsure of what he's trying to do, I rise to my hands and knees. At the same time, I hear his zipper and the rustle of fabric as he quickly undresses.

I let out a gasp of pleasure and shock as I suddenly feel the tip of his cock against my entrance. He rubs against me for a moment, teasing me. And then, without warning, he slides inside me with one deep thrust. The combination of sensations has me bucking against him.

One of his hands comes around to gather my hair, pulling my

head back with a sharp tug. "You're mine," he growls and draws out almost all the way before slamming back in again. "You're mine."

I moan as he pistons into me, bringing me closer and closer to the release he has me begging for.

And over the sounds of our bodies, I'm dimly aware of that strange song playing in the background, omnipresent.

*So sweet, so cold, so fair...*

Thank you for reading! Book 3 coming soon!

# ALSO BY BELLA MOONDRAGON

The Alpha King's Breeder series:

Bought by the Alpha: The Alpha King's Breeder Book 1

Loved by the Alpha: The Alpha King's Breeder Book 2

Lost by the Alpha: The Alpha King's Breeder Book 3

Luna of the Alpha: The Alpha King's Breeder Book 4

Legacy of the Alpha: The Alpha Kings's Breeder Book 5

Daughter of the Alpha: The Alpha King's Breeder Book 6

Descendants of the Alpha: The Alpha King's Breeder Book 7

Shadow of the Alpha: The Alpha King's Breeder Book 8

Son of the Alpha: The Alpha King's Breeder Book 9

The Luna's Vampire Prince series:

The Culling

The Kingdom

The Conquered

Pregnant With Four Alphas' Babies

Chosen As the Breeder

Mated to Four Alphas

Threats Against the Breeder

At War for the Breeder

The Stolen Breeder

Four Alphas, Four Babies

Becoming the Luna Queen

Descendants of the Breeder

Desired by the Devil series

Whispers of the Devil

Banter of the Devil

The Mafia Kings series

Indebted to the Mafia King

<u>Loved by the Mafia King</u>

Claimed by the Mafia King (releases 11/15/2024)

*Sign up for Bella's newsletter here.*

*Follow Bella on Facebook here.*